FENCES

AND

WALLS

 *A Novel*

MELISSA VERDIER

FENCES AND WALLS. By MelissaVerdier.
Copyright © 2017 by Melissa Verdier
Cover design and illustrations by Melissa Verdier

Published by Hunterbrook Press 2017
Stonington, Connecticut, USA
ISBN-978-0-9997600-0-0

Identifiers: 1. Spring, Phoebe (Fictitious character)–Fiction. 2. Maple Ridge (Town)–Fiction. 3. Maple Hill Farm–Fiction.
4. Bipolar–Fiction. 5. Riding–Fiction.
6. Camp Thistle Creek–Fiction. 7. Divorce–Fiction.
8. Up The Creek Country Store–Fiction.

Contact author: mysticverdier17@gmail.com

For Mom and Dad

Many thanks go to Shannon Roberts with The Editorial Department, Donna Good, Tammy Heupel, Bonnie Ryder, Joanne Levy, Joyce Butterfield, Sarah Hansen, the CMB Creative Group, Maura Blaney and Courtney Moore for their assistance.

FENCES AND WALLS

 ## CHAPTER 1 HOME

The tap on my door was hesitant followed by "Phoebe. May I come in?"

I was trying to focus on my English project due Monday, putting the weekend ugly parental scene out of my mind. "What's up, Mom?" I asked.

"I need to talk with you about tonight. It concerns all of us."

I saw that her mascara had run and she'd been crying, her soft blue eyes were red, and blond hair untamed, but she still seemed younger than her thirty-six years. My mom looked so much like Cheryl Ladd they could have been sisters. We called her Charlie's Angel, which often annoyed her. "I am not Kris Monroe, I am Patrice," she would say.

I shrugged, closed the laptop and leaned forward to look out the open window at the June night sky. I thought it would be excellent to be anywhere but here right now.

My mom walked over to the edge of the bed and sat slowly. There was a damp tissue in her hand. Outside, a car door slammed, an engine turned over. The crunching of stones loud at first, then softening in the distance as the car coasted down the driveway.

"I guess you heard the…conversation…downstairs. Your father and I have decided to separate."

I made no reply. Long silence. Shock. Dizzy.

But I want to assure you that everything will work out, PS."

PS is my nickname, short for Phoebe Spring. It's usually meant in a funny way, but the moniker seemed out of place now.

"Daddy will come for you tomorrow after school. He's going to pick you up after tennis and bring you home. Then he's going to be out of town for a little while. On business."

She leaned forward and put her hand on my shoulder. "I want to make this change as smooth as possible for you, Phoebes. It's important you keep studying and involved at school and with your friends. OK?"

Another silence.

"Will we have to move?" I asked.

Mom stared out the window. When she turned to me there was a blank far off look in her eyes that I had never before seen. "Not at this point. No." She waited a bit, gave my shoulder a squeeze and then headed for the door. She half turned and said, "We'll talk about it more tomorrow when you get home."

I can't say the split was a surprise to me. Mom had been seeing a psychiatrist for several years for mild depression, but she'd started acting weirdly, buying all kinds of things she really didn't need. Dad was dealing with it badly and there were so many arguments. Sometimes I just yelled, "PLEASE STOP" to them when the blames got so picky. That's when they decided that I needed a shrink. So now I go by myself to see Dr. Landt. For stress.

I had gotten up after a fitful night's sleep when I heard Mom yelling about something. I pulled on my clothes and ran down to the living room to find her talking to herself while going through boxes of clothing and accessories she had recently bought. She stopped when she saw me come in.

"What's going on, Mom? Aren't you getting ready for work yet?"

She held up a brochure and asked, "What do you think of this color? I'm trading in the Volvo for it."

I was surprised to see a catalog of a silver BMW SUV. I was positive that Dad had no clue she was buying a car, let alone a very expensive one.

"Uh, Mom, maybe you should hold off on this. We just got the Jeep last year."

She said, "The dealer gave me a great price. I'm going to get it. Now do you like the color? I need to know."

I said, "Sure, it looks great, but you look a little wired. Did you ever get to sleep last night?"

"I'm fine. I need to get this done. I don't need sleep now. Go to school."

"Uh, Mom, you're going to be late for work if you don't get ready now. Can I make you some toast?"

"Phoebe, I'm fine. Go outside before you miss the school bus."

I figured I'd better call Dad this morning and let him know he's going to find a big surprise in the driveway.

Sharon Sinks and I usually walked to our first period class together. I closed my locker as I saw her coming to greet me. She was my best friend. We sat together in all our classes either by choice or teacher-assigned alphabetical order. Sinks, Spring. We each had wavy brown hair and brown eyes, but my nose was turned up and a bit longer than hers. We were the same height by an inch. I was five feet three and Sharon, five feet four but opposite sizes. Me: top seven, pants nine. Sharon: top nine, pants seven, making it impossible to trade clothes. My grades were good, and Sharon helped me with my math homework – not my best subject. Our birthdays were one month apart, coming up soon, when we turn fifteen.

"Mom and Dad split up last night," I said. "I called him this morning to find out the big plan."

"Geez, Phoebes, I'm really sorry. What did your Dad say?" she asked.

"I just left a message. He's too busy to talk to me. I'll have to wait until he picks us up after tennis this afternoon. Oh, man. Summer break is in two weeks. Now I'll probably be divided between the two of them. What a mess."

As we watched kids tossing around notes during sixth period English, Sharon whispered, "It's like school is over already to some of these guys. And we still have papers to hand in."

I nodded, "Well, I guess now I have material for my story assignment with all the drama at my house."

After the last period, we walked to our lockers to get our tennis rackets. "Did you study for science yet? I couldn't concentrate on a thing after the blow up."

"I'll get to it after our game today." Sharon added.

We took the ten-minute walk from Maple Ridge High School to the town park where we play tennis. We lobbed a few balls but ended up talking and laughing every time a ball went into the net or over the fence. Mostly mine, as Sharon always humiliates my playing.

I asked Sharon, "Do you feel bad about not seeing your Dad as often?"

"Well, it's better at home now 'cause Mom and I don't argue like we used to 'cause she's not stressed out as much. I wish my dad were still in town like before. I could just go over to his place and have dinner more often. Now that he's in New York, it's a hassle. He's always busy with his girlfriend and doesn't have the time."

I said, "I wonder if I'll still see Dad on the weekends. We used to do things together, but he hasn't been too good on keeping his promises lately. He was supposed to take me to the Yankees in May, and that didn't happen."

We finished our court time, and I looked for his car. His name is Charles. He bought a tricked-out Mini Cooper Countryman last fall for commuting to his law office in Manhattan. He hadn't arrived yet so we sat on a bench with our gear and talked about the summer vacation. A couple of sophomores and juniors were standing by their cars with radios blaring. One of them was doing flips off the hood onto the ground. Two others were pressing park benches over their heads. We just shook our heads at such wasted energy.

We heard someone yell, "Yo, girls. You want some weed?"

We were one week away from an English final ending our freshman year. The last thing I wanted was to complicate my life smoking in the park.

"No thanks. Looks like you guys are doing fine on your own," Sharon answered.

I said, "I guess I'll be home most of the time while Mom's working. But wow, she was really acting weird this morning. Talking to herself and buying more stuff we don't need. I know that was driving Dad crazy."

Mom liked her job at Family Assistance which helped single parents in need. The organization had recently honored her for her dedication and innovative ideas for networking. Last summer I was volunteering there a couple of days a week answering phones and covering reception.

Sharon said, "I'm going to Grams' house for two weeks right after school lets out. And then to my Dad's. He's getting married again next month."

"At least his girlfriend seems OK," I said.

"Yeah, well, her kid, not so much," Sharon added.

"I guess my mom's going to need me around more anyway. Wow, Dad's late. I don't know what happened to him." I took out my phone and called.

Just then I spotted his car pulling up and we gathered our stuff together. Dad's mouth was set in an odd frown. "Hi, girls."

After we dropped off Sharon, I mulled over last night's events. "Did Mom buy that new car today?"

"Uh, well, no, and thanks for the call on that. I'm afraid I have some bad news, Honey."

"What. There's more than you leaving?" I answered sarcastically.

"Your mom, um, needs to be at the hospital for a while. She may have had a breakdown."

What does he mean? The car? Her leg? Financial crisis?

I asked, "What happened?"

"Her office called me this afternoon and said she hadn't come in. I left work early, went to the house, and she, um, anyway, I found she wasn't well, and I had to get her to a hospital. That's why I was late. She's at Westchester Medical."

I was trying to process this news, as Dad turned into our driveway on Long Meadow Road. We parked in front of the garage of our colonial style house.

I was staring at the pretty copse of trees in the backyard, but an image of Mom at the hospital was stuck in my head. "Aren't we going to see her now?"

Dad sat with his hands on the steering wheel, looked at me and replied, "Not yet, but hopefully soon. She needs a little time for the doctors to do a complete check up before you can go."

"What's wrong with her?" I asked. "She's been acting so strange lately. I mean sometimes she's really aggravated about work, and the next day she's either hopped up about something or she won't get out of bed."

"You know the medications for depression she's been on? They're no longer working for her. Her doctor and I have been very concerned about the way she's been acting, and she may have to go to a different hospital. We have to wait and see what the doctor says."

"Oh."

"This is a different kind of illness than you may be thinking."

"What do you mean?"

"Again, she needs to have a complete medical workup, both physically and mentally. We have to work together on this, you understand." He stated. "I know that it's going to be difficult for you, and I will be only a phone call away."

"I don't get it, Dad. You're still moving out? What about me?"

"I can't be here for you right now, Phoebe, as your mom always has been. So I contacted Ellen Sinks, and she has agreed to have you stay for the next two weeks with Sharon until school is over."

"But, Dad…"

13

"Phoebe, listen. I have a case I'm currently working on and need to be in New York for longer hours. That's why I can't stay here all the time. When I'm here on the weekends, you'll come back home and we'll be together."

I felt the tears coming and the breath being sucked out of my chest. I had so many questions, and I felt that Dad wasn't telling me everything. He was leaving me behind.

"But where are you staying in the city?"

"A co-worker is putting me up for the time being. I'm in the middle of this case, and I can't hand it off to anyone. So we have to deal with what we have in front of us...OK?" He continued, "We stay here tonight – you can get some things together for the remainder of the week, and we'll drop off your bags at the Sinks' on the way to school tomorrow."

Burning with tears, I went inside our house. The moment I opened the door, I saw that our orderly home was trashed. A lamp was overturned and dishes were on the kitchen floor with some other new items Mom had just purchased thrown around.

"Oh, my gosh! Was there a break-in here?"

"No, Phoebes, your mom did this."

"Were you here when all this happened?"

"For part of it. Your mom became very angry about my canceling the new car and was so agitated, I was worried for her safety. That's when I called her doctor, and he arranged for her hospital admittance."

He quickly added, "I'm sorry, Honey, I'll get this cleaned up right away, I didn't have time earlier."

"Dad. I'll help." The confusion just brought more tears. How did Mom go from depressed to crazy? An image of calm Mom was clear in my head, not in the way he described. How did I miss her being so sick that she'd wreck the house?

After we swept up the broken plates and emptied the trash, Dad fixed spaghetti for us. He poured himself a drink, which was very unusual for a weeknight. We ate quietly in the kitchen.

Dad looked to me. "You know she's been on pills for depression for a couple of years. We've been to counseling. I've tried to help her. Unfortunately, we can't seem to live together. I don't know why I make her worse, but I do."

"I haven't been able to help either," I said, feeling my eyes burning again.

"Actually, Phoebe, you do give her the stability that she needs. You're the one who's kept her focused, but she's just reached a breaking point. She needs serious professional help."

Sadly, as I grabbed a tissue, I picked up the family photo of the three of us together at Yosemite, bringing a jolt from the past when I thought everything was perfect.

Dad said softly, "I'd like you to please continue your appointments with Dr. Landt to have someone to talk to."

"This is the week we're supposed to go together. Remember you said you'd go with me to see her?"

"I didn't forget. I'll make sure you get there," he nodded.

I cleaned the dishes and headed upstairs to my homework wondering if Mom was OK. My thoughts kept going off course from my English assignment to what was happening here. Separation? Divorce? Breakdown? I found a duffle and loaded some clean clothes and toiletries I'd need for the week at Sharon's. Then I gave up on my homework, set my alarm and pulled back the covers to try to sleep. I listened to the peepers outside advertising for mates in our pond. It's a very soothing, nighttime country sound. I finally drifted off.

Good thing I'd gotten everything packed Monday night because the next morning I woke up to Dad calling for me. I'd hit the snooze setting on the alarm. He assured me he'd leave a text message on any updates after we dropped off my bag at Sharon's on the way to school.

The day was a disaster from the start. I didn't hear my English teacher call my name to read my short narrative that I was unable to finish two nights ago. I dozed off momentarily during algebra until my book fell to the floor with a loud WHAP. I finally woke up during Living Environment. At least there I learned enough about the life process of cells and zygotes to write a novel.

As Sharon and I walked to the cafeteria, she bumped my arm. "Mom told me you're going to stay with us?"

I said, "I can't talk now. Later, OK?" We collected our choices and headed for the dessert section. I nervously grabbed three just-baked chocolate chip cookies and finished one of them by the time we sat down.

Maple Ridge is a really small community and everyone knows everybody. Brian Wykoff walked over to our table saying, "Hey, Phoebe. I heard about a police call to your house yesterday. What happened?"

I remembered that his dad's a local cop. The blood rushed to my head, and I knew I was blushing horribly. And my dad didn't think to mention this? I realized my mouth was hanging open stupidly.

"Uh, Brian, could you keep that to yourself, please?" I looked around wildly to see if anyone else heard what he said. "I really don't want to talk about it to anyone."

"Jeez, Phoebe, I only meant to see if you were OK. I didn't mean anything by it. I'm not telling anybody," he said defensively.

"Well, please don't," I implored. "To anyone."

He walked away quickly.

Sharon looked confused. "Oh, my gosh, Phoebe? What happened?"

"There was an incident. I'll tell you later."

I was so pissed that Dad didn't tell me anything about the police. And she needed an ambulance too? Then I realized if Brian knew, there are a couple of other EMT and cops' kids in school. The barn door was wide open now.

I went to my locker to check my phone. We weren't supposed to use them during school hours, but I figured, hey, my mom probably was arrested, seemed to be in the cracker factory, so what's a teacher going to say to me? No calls or messages yet. Finally at two thirty, when Sharon and I were on our way to art club, my phone buzzed.

"Hi, Dad."

"How was your day, Phoebes?"

"Not so good, Dad. Why couldn't you tell me that the police and EMTs were at the house yesterday? It seems I'm the only one at school who didn't know."

"I'm not in a place where I can go into that right now, Honey. Yes, it was a serious situation, and Mom is going to remain at least a few days at Westchester Medical before any transfer occurs. Her doctor wants her settled there before you go to see her. She knows you are asking about her, which is important. OK?"

"Dad, when are you coming back home?"

"I'll be there Saturday morning. I can pick you up at the Sinks around eleven."

"OK, you'll call me?"

"Bye, Phoebe," and he cut me off again.

I caught up with Sharon in art and continued on a drawing from the other day. It was a study of a bird in a cage. I hadn't thought it to be symbolic when I started it, but should birds be enclosed in a little space behind bars? I wanted it to be different, so I finished the drawing with the cage door ajar. For the last

19

forty minutes, I'd been so focused on the pencil and charcoal, my mind was cleared of distractions. Slowly, my chaotic problems emerged in real time again. I tucked the drawing in my portfolio, and we cleaned up fast before running to the late bus in time to get dropped at Sharon's.

Mrs. Sinks wasn't back from showing a house yet, so we made a fruit snack and sat at the kitchen table while I told Sharon what was going on.

I couldn't believe how hard it was to put Mom's situation into words. I wanted to blame someone. There must have been something we could have done to help her before it got to the men in white coats stage. I was sure my mom could snap out of the mental state that Dad had described. She could handle anything.

"You know, Shar, I don't know where I'd be right now if it weren't for your mom. Dad's so involved at work he can't take the time to be home. So here I am."

"But, Phoebe, someone's got to pay the bills. Give your dad a little credit for dealing with this situation. Besides, I like having a roommate."

"He just dismisses me. Clams up," I griped as I reached for a tissue. "He'd just moved out to be rid of the drama at home, and wham, about the worst scenario possible just landed in his lap. If he trusted me, I could help."

Sharon countered, "That's how parents are. They keep things from their kids to protect them from whatever. Financial worries, health issues, scary demons. That's their job."

"But he should be truthful about what's happening. Especially when it's Mom."

Sharon picked up her book for our algebra homework when my phone rang. It read Unavailable. I wondered if it could be the hospital calling me so I tapped Accept to hear silence. Then a low girl's voice said, "You know your mom's crazy. It runs in the family."

I slammed my thumb to cancel the call. Sharon looked at me, surprised.

I said, "Hate calls in the making already. Great."

"Do you know who that was?"

I scrunched up my face. "I'm not sure, but it may have been Jackie Lorrenze."

Sharon frowned, "You drew that cartoon of her bent over with words coming out of her butt last year! Then you put it up on the school bulletin board? Jeez, that was kind of harsh," as she made a duck face.

"Well, I didn't start that mess, Jackie did, when she posted all those nasty things about me on Facebook and Instagram. That's how the principal got involved. For the cyber-bullying."

Sharon pointed out, "She didn't like your moving in on her guy crush at Randy's party. I was there with Jackie, and boy, she was pissed at you, falling all over him."

"I beg your pardon, missy. Why is it when a girl does a little making out with a guy, she's a 'ho, but when a guy makes out with a girl, he's a sly dude?" I asked. "And besides, I wasn't drunk, and I didn't know she liked him. I mean, she was my best friend then, so I don't know why she never told me."

"What finally went down after you did the drawing?" Sharon asked.

"My mom and Jackie's mom are really good friends, so they wanted everything patched up. Then at the meeting with the principal, that's when my mom found out about the drinking party that started the whole hot mess. Mom was like, 'So disappointed with you, Phoebe, no more parties. I won't tell Daddy as long as it doesn't happen again,' and that was supposed to end it." I mimicked.

"I'm surprised you remember anything about that night."

"Oh, my God, I only shared two vodkas with that guy and nothing else happened. I don't know why Jackie got so mad. It wasn't my fault he liked me."

"I'm glad you don't go to all those wild parties anymore. Too many bad things happen when everybody gets wasted. Like when that junior got alcohol poisoning in April," said Sharon.

"Yeah, that was horrible. But why is Jackie starting in on me again? I didn't do anything to her now. And I really hate that people know about my mom."

We finished our homework together. At least at Sharon's, I could forget the distractions.

"Hi, Mrs. Sinks." I said, as she walked into the kitchen carrying groceries. "I hope I won't be in the way here."

"Phoebe, you're welcome any time, you know. Can you girls put the food away while I change? Then we'll have dinner together."

We cleared our books from the table and prepared a salad while Mrs. Sinks was upstairs. She came down in blue pants and coral top that complimented her fair complexion and figure. She wore her brown hair shoulder length in a pretty bob.

"Are you girls prepared for your finals?"

"That's what we're doing tonight, Mom. Along with Phoebe's math review," as she smacked my arm.

We were setting the dinner table when Mrs. Sinks said, "Phoebe, I spoke with your father earlier. I'll be taking you to your doctor appointment tomorrow."

"Wait a minute. You mean he's not coming to the appointment? I thought that was the plan. He said he'd be there."

"I'm sorry, Phoebe, Charles said he had to work."

23

"But he promised to go with me to my shrink. Dad should be there, don't you think? I have so many questions and no answers, and they won't even let me see Mom or even talk to her."

I remembered the complete mess she made of our house. I still couldn't believe that she'd lose control like that. And when school's over, would she be coming home? And Dad's not going to be around, so he should be stepping up now to be prepared for her leaving the hospital.

Mrs. Sinks said, "Come sit down for a second, Phoebe," as I took the chair next to her. Her serious look showed her concern. "Even incredibly bright and talented people like Patrice can be overwhelmed by moments that other people work through easily. You have every reason to feel left out of Patrice's healing process right now, but let the professionals get started on a proper evaluation first. Then the family can get involved with what the doctors prescribe."

"I can't help wishing there was something I could have done."

"No, my dear. In this case, neither you nor anyone could have helped, and you are in no way to blame for what's happened. And don't underestimate your role in getting her back home. Just try to have patience with your dad. Patrice is in good professional hands, but it may take time to zero in on the correct treatment."

"I really miss her."

"I'd be worried if you didn't."

We finished dinner, and Sharon and I cleaned the kitchen.

Mrs. Sinks said, "If you'd like, I can probably take you both to the stable on Friday after school."

I nodded yes to Sharon, and she said, "That would be great, Mom."

Mrs. Sinks said, "You know, I used to ride in high school. Haven't gone in years, but I still have my riding gear."

Sharon said, "I think the styles have changed since you rode, Mom. They don't wear those real baggie breeches anymore."

Sharon's mom said, "If you're thinking of those safari looking pants that went out in the sixties, that's way before my time, young lady."

Sharon had a trundle bed that her mom pulled out and made up for me. I hung up the few clothes I brought for the remainder of the week and put on my lucky penguin pjs.

Sharon said, "Don't you want to call your dad tonight?"

"No, not now. He won't share anything anyway." I lay in bed trying to trace Mom's strange behavior to when it first became a real problem. What was it that put her over the edge? She was doing OK a year ago during that drinking party/Jackie incident. Then, I remembered not too much later, her doctor appointments became more frequent. She didn't start complaining about work until fairly recently. Around that time Dad and Mom started to really lose it when they were together. My eyes were so heavy. I couldn't think any more. I drifted off.

I woke up Wednesday morning with Sharon's poodle, Jasmine, tucked under my nose. She's curly and white. She looked so comfy, but I woke her with a little nudge. "Time to get up," tickling her soft head.

Then I remembered. "Hey, there, birthday girl. Wake up!" to Sharon as she pulled the covers back. We went downstairs to Mrs. Sinks greeting us with homemade waffles and whipped cream. "Happy birthday, my darling daughter. For you on this special fifteenth birthday."

Sharon threw her mom a kiss. "Wow, thanks to the best mom ever," as we dug in. We each had two.

I just hoped for a low-key day. We finished getting ready and waited outside for the school bus.

Sharon said, "Phoebe, look. That's your dad driving by."

He didn't see us standing in the driveway. Why was he here in Maple Ridge this morning? Why didn't he call me? What the hell?

I was prepared for all of my classes today. There was a vocab test in French and a discussion in English on narrative vs. expository writing. My mind kept picturing where Mom was—

in a bed or a cold hospital room? I just could not get that image out of my head.

After the last class, Mrs. Sinks was waiting to take Sharon home and me to my shrink's office. Dr. Landt initially worked as a high school guidance counselor and left that job to start her own private practice.

"Hi, Phoebe, come in," Dr. Landt said.

So far, I wasn't too successful putting my feelings into words. Now I had fear on top of anxiety from Mom in the hospital. My last session was weeks before Mom's episode, and now I felt the emotions rising in my chest. I willed myself not to cry at first, and the words I'd been holding back spilled out quickly.

"Mom seemed so calm the night Dad left, like it was no big deal. I was just going to keep my grades up, and everything would be the same except Dad wouldn't be living with us, but she had this weird unfocused glaze in her eyes. She wouldn't look at me. She just stared off into space."

Dr. Landt asked, "Phoebe, can you tell me what is more upsetting? Your father's leaving or your mom's breakdown?"

"I think I could handle one or the other but not both things. Dad says he'll come and help, but then he just stays in the city working on some case. I feel helpless to help her," I grabbed a tissue. "I had no idea that she was so sick. I just thought she needed a couple more pills or something."

"Do you feel this is your responsibility?"

"Well, who else is going to take care of her when she's ready to come home again?"

Dr. Landt waited for a minute before speaking. "You are dealing with an awful situation, but your mom's illness and the divorce you alone can't fix."

"But I'm angry. I don't know why. It's not her fault."

"Yes, you are angry. I can see it in your posture, I can hear it in your voice. I'd like you to close your eyes, and let's go back to the night that your mom told you about the separation and your first reaction."

I leaned back and tried to unclench my hands. "I felt almost relieved," I sighed. "They'd been arguing so much, and I missed how we used to do things together and go places. At first I thought it must be Mom's fault."

"Why's that?"

"Because I couldn't understand the buying spree. Dad was really upset with her about it. She was always so...sensible about money before."

Dr. Landt said, "Let's stop for a moment. You felt that something else was wrong when she was unable to stop spending money."

"Yes, I guess."

"Your dad called me and explained what has happened. The doctor currently working with her feels your mom is bipolar. There will be more evaluations, but I'm telling you this now so that you can understand that the erratic up and down behavior is part of her illness. You didn't make it worse – in fact your mom was more than likely trying to keep it together for you."

"Is she going to get better?" I asked realizing that Dr. Landt was trying to remove my guilt.

"It will take some time, as I'm sure your dad said, but yes, I do believe she will."

"But I was blaming her for being weak. That she's supposed to be able to handle problems. I didn't help because I just kept telling her to take more pills. I had no idea what she was dealing with. I didn't know. She was taking too many and no one said anything."

"You aren't responsible, Phoebe." She handed me the tissue box. "Sometimes medications just don't work. For your mom, unfortunately, there was a breaking point. Next week, you and I should try some relaxation methods to help you with the anxiety you're clearly feeling."

I left the office feeling wrung out, face bloated and hot from crying, but at least I found out a name for what Mom was going through. Bipolar. Something else on the research list.

On our way back to the house, Mrs. Sinks stopped to buy a big pizza to bring home for Sharon's birthday. As soon as I got in the door, my phone buzzed. This time I didn't answer it, but I could see that a message was left. I played it on speaker for Sharon to hear.

"Your mom's a nut case, and your Dad's a liar." I shut it down. "What's with the freaking name calling?" I said. I was getting fed up with it.

Sharon glanced sideways as I was ripping the lettuce apart for our salad, "Whoa, girl, take it easy on the green leaf. You don't have to attack it."

"I'm so miffed about these calls. I hate this spying and lying about us. Makes no sense."

"Someone at school will know for sure if it's Jackie. I'll bet she isn't keeping it to herself. We'll ask around this week."

Sharon opened four presents after dinner. Her mom gave her a pretty circle pendant with a tiny diamond on a gold chain. Her dad and Grams both gave her checks with really funny cards, and from me, a pretty silver bracelet I knew she liked. Mrs. Sinks brought out the ice cream birthday cake with fifteen candles and said to Sharon, "I'd like to take you shopping next week for summer clothes."

Upstairs, I researched bipolar on my laptop and found so many things Mom was doing. Needing less sleep, ranges in emotions from excitement to no interest at all. Hyper, lavish spending. It made sense now.

I called Dad and he picked up right away.

He said, "I was just going to call you. You OK, Honey?"

I said, "Dr. Landt explained Mom's diagnosis to me. I wish you would've told me first. I looked up 'bipolar' and a lot of what Mom was doing is included."

"Yes, the spending is one of the problems. I wasn't sure if bipolar is definite, but it fits. I have to ask you to please find her bank records, because I'm pretty sure her account is overdrawn. Can you get them for me when you go home? They're in the file cabinet in the office. I don't know where her checkbook is."

"OK, I'll find them."

On Thursday we took the bus to Sharon's and worked on the last of our studying. We had pasta ready for an early dinner together when another call came in on my cell. I let it go to voicemail. "Someone should lock up your pathetic family in the crazy house and never let you out."

Mrs. Sinks was shocked. "You should keep a record of any calls like that."

I nodded. "I'm transferring them to my computer. And now I have to confront her."

Sharon warned, "Before you do, have a back up plan. She's a giant, remember."

My mom usually took Sharon and me to the stable every Friday after school, but this time Mrs. Sinks had offered to drive us. She picked us up right at two twenty dismissal while she was on a late lunch break. I was looking forward to it all day. We changed into our jeans and chaps at Sharon's and grabbed our helmets on our way to Mrs. Sinks's car.

There are three barns for both private and school horses, an indoor ring, and a good sized outdoor ring that they maintain well. The school horses were ridden so much that us barn regulars were given permission from a few of the owners to ride their private horses. We usually booked the ones needing exercise for a two-hour hack to Swan Lake and beyond. We said hi to the barn manager, Doris Kingsley, when she saw us checking over Jasper and Woodstock.

After we finished tacking up their English saddles, we made our way toward the path to the trails. Maple Hill Farm is adjacent to the Rockefeller State Park and Preserve. The cinder trails were installed decades ago by the Rockefeller family, and were designed to be very wide for carriages to pass. The trails wind along streams and meadows in the Park for 150 miles between Pleasantville, Sleepy Hollow, and Tarrytown, with fantastic views of the Hudson River.

I had to avoid talking about Mom's condition today. Too upsetting to discuss, and there were other problems pending. We started up the long hill toward one of the bridal paths. "I think Jackie is confused. Why would she start an attack on Dad now?" I complained.

Sharon replied, "I know people have grudges, but after a year's gone by, that's just nuts."

"Should I call Mrs. Lorrenze about what's going on? Jackie's a loose screw now. I don't want an explosion."

"Maybe that's the way to go. You can't ask your mom."

We paused the horses at Swan Lake to look at the ducks and geese. I broke the momentary silence explaining, "Dr. Landt told me how I shouldn't feel responsible for Mom, but I just can't agree. I guess Dad's talking to the doctors. I'm calling him again today because he didn't pick up last night. My father is just avoiding me."

Sharon said, "It must be so hard to have the person you depend on all of a sudden become the dependent one, and you can't make any decisions."

"That's what's so frustrating. Dr. Landt's at least being up front with what's wrong, bipolar and all. But not my dad. I feel left out."

Just then, a fox not usually out at this time of day, was walking up ahead carrying a prize in her mouth for her kits. She glanced back at us and trotted off to the woods. Sharon eased Jasper into an effortless canter encouraging a competition with Woodstock who picked up his own pace. We breezed along – our hair flipping rhythmically with every canter stride, then slowed toward one of the paths that intersects with Bedford Road. We trotted toward the Union Church of Pocantico Hills when I asked Sharon, "Would you mind waiting for me? I haven't been here since last Christmas with Mom and Dad."

Sharon nodded as she took Woodstock's reins. "Take your time, Phoebes. It's a good place to clear your head."

I had seen photos of Mom and Dad's wedding here, and we used to go together for Sunday services. I always found it to be kind of settling, maybe because of the small size and the sunny stained glass. You'd think you were in a museum the first time you saw the beautiful Henri Matisse rose window above the altar, and the eight prophets and angels along the nave by Marc Chagall. My favorite among them was always Ezekiel reaching for God's book. But the major work was the ninth window of the Good Samaritan from the New Testament, and that filled almost the entire back wall with color and light.

I sat in the back pew looking at how the sunlight played with the deep blues and emerald greens of the glass. My art teacher explained to me how Chagall's acid wash and double layers of paint made the colors so different. So few people knew of this church, which made it even more special.

I remembered so clearly walking in behind Mom and Dad for a Sunday church service when we were all together. I felt more uplifted, and left the church to join Sharon and Woodstock.

Sharon gestured, "We should turn back now." I cut ahead of Sharon and led us toward a path bordering the farm on the property when I heard someone coming up fast from behind. I yelled, "Slow down!" to the rider as her horse galloped past us kicking up stones. The look on the girl's face signaled she was in trouble. Sharon and I quickly rode after her with Woodstock catching up to her left side and Jasper to the right side of her horse. Sharon leaned in to grab the reins as our horses settled the runaway into a trot and walk.

"Holy cow, thanks," the girl said. "I was going back to Maple Hill and walked into a couple of bees about a half-mile back, and he was stung. He bolted and I couldn't stop."

There was no swelling, so the three of us cooled off the horses with the half-mile walk back to Maple Hill. We gave Gunsmoke to Jerry, the groom, explained to him what happened, and the girl went to the office to see Doris.

Sharon and I retrieved halters, took bridles, saddles and pads back to their proper places, finished brushing out coats, and checked hooves. The groom took Jasper and Woodstock to their stalls where water, oats and hay were waiting. We hung out in the office chatting with Doris until we saw Mrs. Sinks pull in.

She said to us, "Next time, I think I want to come with you. It's been too long. I miss this place."

"We'll take it easy on you and spare your gluteus maximus," said Sharon.

"Ah, yes. The sore-butt syndrome. Remind me to take a saddle pad."

We arrived at Sharon's when my phone rang.

I picked up. "Dad, what time are you coming Saturday?"

"I can't make it Saturday morning. I've called your brother, and he'll be coming to pick you up at the Sinks'. Your mother has been transferred to a hospital in White Plains."

"But Dad. You promised you'd be here."

"I know. I'm very sorry. That's why I called Drew to pick you up early. This way you'll get to see her and you won't have to wait any longer."

"Please, Dad. Isn't there any way you can come with me to the hospital?"

"Not this time, Sweetie. But, I was thinking that you should go home to pack some clean things for Mom to take with you. Please pick out some tops and underwear for her when you stop at the house. When is your next appointment with Dr. Landt?" he asked.

"I'm supposed to go back next week. Dad, I'm getting strange calls on the phone about Mom and you."

He said nothing at first. "What is this? Who is calling you?"

"I'm not sure, but I think it's Jackie Lorrenze."

Silence. "Dad?"

"If it happens again, please tell me," he said.

We hung up. I'm not sure how or why Drew was called in to this. It would seem that his job interviews following his graduation from Lehigh University have turned up nothing solid, so he was able to help out with "Patrice's problem."

Dad's first wife was Darleen. Drew is their son and he currently lives in Greenwich, Connecticut. In other words, Drew is my half-brother from Mother #1. He's twenty-two and we barely know each other.

CHAPTER 3 ACCUSATIONS

Saturday morning, Drew Spring entered the Sinks' driveway at ten thirty. At five feet ten with wavy, almost black hair and brown eyes, he was like a twin for Dad. Same father as me, but the only resemblance is our eyes. My face is rounder, where Drew's is chiseled.

I wore what I had on Friday for school feeling pretty cool as I stepped in his car. As a nod for making it through four years of non-stop partying, Dad and Darleen bought him a silver 2014 A4 Audi with only 18,000 miles on the odometer. I had to admit I was impressed.

On our way to my house, I asked, "How about a driving lesson later on?"

Drew raised an eyebrow and looked at me for a second as we turned into the driveway. "You're fourteen, and it's a manual transmission."

"What?" I said. "I can drive. Dad gave me lessons on the Mini lots of times. He says every girl should learn on a standard shift. You never know when it might come in handy."

"Don't hold your breath," he said as we pulled up to the garage.

I gasped instead. PSYCHO MOM was painted in big white letters on the side of my house.

"What the hell?" Drew exclaimed.

In shock I said, "Someone's leaving me hate messages too, and I think I know who it is. But this? This is too much!"

I was shaking with anger when I unlocked the door. Drew took a photo of it and went to the garage to find some house paint while I started looking for the things I needed to take to Mom. I changed my jeans and headed for the car. I stomped out to take another look at the graffiti, grabbed the paintbrush Drew found and winged it into the side of the house. "How dare she do this to us? I'm not putting up with this crap."

He said, "I'll take care of it today, but I'm calling the police first."

"Wait, Drew. It's bad enough that a few people know my mom's sick, but I don't want the WHOLE town to read it in the newspaper."

"I'm keeping photos of it, and you need to save the calls being made to you, too, in case this escalates. I'm serious, Phoebe."

When we got to the hospital, we entered the Psychiatric Unit. Holy cow. Reality sucks. We checked in at the nurse's office and asked if Mom's fresh clothes could be taken to her closet. The nurse directed us to the end of the hall to a large room. Prior to the visit, I had imagined her in a gloomy, depressing place, but I was surprised to find the community area was nicely furnished with comfortable sitting nooks and card tables. Tall windows let the sunlight reflect against the softly painted beige walls and polished white floor tiles. Mom was sitting on a small couch reading a paperback.

"Oh Phoebe, it's about time you arrived. I've been waiting since this morning. I have nothing to wear. Did you bring some clothes for me? Although I won't need them, really. I'm going to be leaving next week."

"Hi, Mom," I gave her a big hug. "Yes, I gave your clothes to the nurse." Then added, "Drew and I can sit with you on the couch." I saw the book in her hand. "What are you reading now?"

She said, "Oh, I already finished this."

"What's it about?"

"I don't know. I don't remember," as Mom looked toward the door. "Have you come to take me home? Let me get my things so we can leave. I shouldn't be here, you know. It's all a mistake. Your father put me here just because I bought a few things. Did you bring that sweater? I wanted you to bring the one that just arrived the other day. It's too cold here. I need something warmer."

I had no idea what to do with Mom's rambling sentences. It was hard to see her so mixed up. "Drew and I came by to talk to you about your treatment."

"Well, I can tell you about my treatment at work. I've made some great suggestions at Family Assistance, and they aren't following through with them. I made that organization a success, and they just don't appreciate what I've done. They don't do networking properly. If it hadn't been for me, the place would have been bankrupt years ago."

Mom did the accounting at Family Assistance, and she kept excellent records. She worked closely with Barbara Lorrenze who did much of the fund raising. I'd never heard Mom talk this way before about the organization she loved so much.

I could feel the sweat on my face dripping. She was so much worse than I expected. How do you talk to someone who isn't listening? "Mom, school is almost over, and I think I may make the honor roll as long as I can keep my math grade up."

"Well, of course you will. Did I tell you the doctor said I'm going home next week? I don't like it here. They won't let me sleep in the morning. I just need rest. I keep telling the nurses this, and they still make me get up so early. I'm so tired."

I looked at Drew for help and he finally said, "But, Patrice, your best quality is helping people, and now the nurses want to help you get better quickly, so you can go home."

"Yes, I have always helped everyone," she said, looking around.

We hugged as we stood up, but Mom's face melted into tears when I turned to leave.

I handed her some tissues, but instead of taking them, she pointed to Drew and said, "There is the Devil."

Drew was completely blind-sided with that and took a few steps back. Mom was still confused and mistook Drew for Dad's younger self.

"No, Mom, this is Drew. He cares about you just as much as I do."

She was silent, but seemed to recognize her mistake. "Oh, my God, you look so much like Charles," she said.

"I'll be back in a few days, Mom, I promise. Can you please listen to what the doctors are asking of you? You'll get better so quickly if you do."

"I'm fine, really, Phoebe."

She started to say something and then broke down in tears again.

"I just can't face another day here. Promise that you'll get me out. Don't listen to your father. Don't listen to anything he tells you."

I handed her some more tissues wondering why she was so afraid of what Dad would say. Our exit did not go well. She collapsed in a chair crying, and I quickly went back to her knowing how it felt to be forgotten. "It's OK, Mom. Remember, we're thinking about how much stronger you'll feel the next visit. Everyone here wants to help you too."

We left the community area, and were shown to the doctor's office. Dr. Gordon looked up from his notes. "Unfortunately, Drew and Phoebe, I'm sorry to tell you that Mrs. Spring is quite ill as you may have seen this morning. She is confusing facts with fantasy as well as denying any need for therapy at this point, and she should receive hospital care until we have addressed these issues."

My stomach just dropped.

He went on, "I relayed information on your mother's condition to Mr. Spring yesterday. There are certain bipolar medications that are extremely effective for most people. I am confident that with the adjustment in her medication and continued therapy, she'll improve."

"How long are we looking at, Dr. Gordon?" Drew asked.

He said, "It's never an overnight process. But again, I'm hopeful that you should see a difference in a couple of weeks. That does not mean that she will be ready for home. Once released, it's very important she continue her medication, as there is no current bipolar cure."

Drew and I walked to the car. I was physically shaking with the realization that Mom needed a lot more help than the family alone could provide. He sat behind the wheel and didn't say anything for a full minute. "I'm sorry you have to go through this. I'll paint over the house graffiti when I take you home, and then I have some errands to run, but I'll be back this afternoon."

Drew picked me up later for dinner at an Italian restaurant in Millwood, where, surprise, Dad was waiting for us. "Phoebe, I hope you're not upset that I didn't go with you today. I wanted to take you, but the doctor felt that my presence would just exacerbate the situation due to our separation."

"She looked awful, Dad. She was so down and spaced-out and totally confused. I didn't know what to do or say. I asked you to come with me. At least you could tell me what's going on before I hear it from someone else."

Angrily, he retorted, "Now just wait a minute, Phoebe. I'm doing what the doctor is recommending. I know this is a horrible situation, but you and I need to work together. I certainly want what's best for Patrice, and right now, I'm also counting on you and Drew."

"Well, maybe if you called more, I'd know what is expected."

Drew cut in to clear the air. "You sell yourself short, Phoebe. You helped her today. You saw that she opened up talking to you."

"How am I supposed to help? She wasn't acting herself at all and now you're going to stay in the city all summer, right Dad?"

"Please, calm down. That's what I want to talk to you about. I know how much you like riding and sports. I found a camp in Massachusetts that offers all of that. You'd be riding every day and enjoying the things you love to do. I can arrange for you to go there for the summer. Do you think that would be something you'd like?"

"Isn't it too late to sign up at a camp?"

"I phoned them today and they have an opening in your age group. Someone canceled at the last minute. You can stay home for one week with Drew at the house or with Mrs. Sinks and then leave June 30. It would be Camp Thistle Creek's full seven-week session. Here is the brochure and the website you can look up on your phone."

I immediately shot Drew with my squinty-eyed look wondering if he'd brought up the idea of sending me away. They were worried I'd do something stupid if left on my own. My hands were clenched tight, knowing in the end I probably wouldn't have a say whether I wanted to leave or stay.

"But I wouldn't be able to see Mom or help like you said. And who'd look after the house?"

Dad reasoned, "If you're at camp, won't it be better than sitting around here waiting to see Mom and still not be able to

45

help? Phoebes, she's going to be there for some time. You can Facetime with the doctor's permission. Remember, her medication has to be monitored closely before any progress is made."

Drew cut in. "I checked out the camp, too. It would be a great chance for you to meet some other girls who like riding as much as you. I can take you to Massachusetts if you want. I have a buddy over that way I can see."

Loudly, I complained, "It's not fair being left out, Dad. I feel like you're pushing me away and just deciding things for me."

"Phoebe, the last thing I want is to see you pacing circles around the house thinking you're somehow responsible for your mom's health. Please go and have a good summer."

With both Dad and Drew on my case and Mom not here to back me up, I knew the decision was made. I was going to Camp Thistle Creek.

Sunday morning, Drew had left for Greenwich and wouldn't be back to Maple Ridge till Monday afternoon. I was angrily pacing the house when Sharon showed up.

"Hey," she greeted brightly, as I opened the door to let her in. "Do you want some company? Drew called to say you needed cheering up. So I told my mom that I was going to stay with you tonight and help choose your clothes for camp."

"I'm so glad you're here. I need to vent, big time." I yelled. "First, the phone messages, and then yesterday I found 'Psycho Mom' painted on the side of the house."

Sharon nearly choked. "WHAT? Do you think Jackie did that?"

"Who else knows? And she's the only one leaving the messages. Then Dad really upset me yesterday. It's like he can't take the time to talk. He sent Drew as a buffer."

Sharon said, "I know – that's how I felt when my father took off last year. I was really mad."

"Then let's go to the city today. I really need the distraction, and we could go to MOMA or the Metropolitan and get to see their new exhibitions." I added, "Pleeease?"

She hesitated, "I told my mom we were going to study."

"We'd be back by dinner tonight in case your Mom calls," tempting her.

Sharon pulled up the Scarborough Station train schedule on her phone. "Here it is. Train at one or two o'clock."

I said jumping up, "We can catch the two o'clock. It takes twenty-five minutes to walk from here."

"Okay. Let's get to it, but I only have thirty-three dollars. Not enough for train or food or entry anywhere."

"Mom keeps cash around the house. Let me see if I can find some."

I went to her underwear drawer and found $100.00. Then I checked a couple of places in the office and found another $150.00. I counted what was in my wallet and it came to $280.00. I had one credit card with a parent-imposed limit of $100.00. Good to go. I tucked the cash in a money pouch that I wear around my waist. Better safe than sorry.

Sharon borrowed a pair of slacks from my Mom's closet, and I changed into slacks and a decent shirt. We had a light lunch before straightening up my room and set out for the station.

We only had a five-minute wait for the train and took a seat on the side that had the Hudson River view. Once we arrived at Grand Central, we walked to the Forty-second Street exit to find that the queue for the taxis wasn't long. That would be the quickest way to get to MOMA and could give us time to see a couple of exhibits before the museum closed at five thirty.

I said, "Lets go to the 'Women Artists and Postwar Abstraction' exhibit. That's the one our art teacher was talking about last week."

We climbed into the car as I said to the driver, "Eleven West Fifty-third, please." It was a newer taxi, I noticed, kind of similar to the taxicab–TV game show with two seats in the middle and two behind but without all the lights and cash winning fun.

There was just a short line to enter the museum, and we went to the members' desk. I presented our family membership card and asked for the exhibit locations. Sharon hadn't been to MOMA before, so we casually walked by more galleries before reaching the Women's exhibit. We picked out two paintings and pointed out the elements we both liked. After forty minutes there, we went on to find the Ian Cheng: Emissaries gallery.

"Oh, my gosh," Sharon said…"I didn't expect this at all. It's like a video game. And it's playing itself! See, over there," she motioned.

We were staring at a futuristic end-of-the-world scene of a bombed-out town. The artist had created groups of surreal animated people carrying supplies around a destroyed village.

"This is like Disney on LSD. Wow. I can't look away." I remarked.

Five-thirty came too quickly. Sharon and I stood at the corner at Fifth Avenue and Fifty-third Street waiting for the light. We took in the grit of the city, the constant traffic noise, people walking with a purpose while talking on their cell phones, and I knew what to do. "I think we should go down to Greenwich Village to one of the jazz clubs Drew told me about."

Sharon didn't even hesitate. "Good plan. Lead the way."

We headed south on Fifth Avenue and browsed in Victoria's Secret, then continued walking until we stood in front of St. Patrick's Cathedral at Fiftieth Street. After admiring the enormous bronze statue of Atlas, I pointed, "Let's cut in here to Rockefeller Center." We strolled by the busy café at the Summer Garden to the gilded statue of Prometheus feeling the cool spray of the surrounding fountain.

I said, "Dad took me here for skating last December. That was the last time we had a nice day together."

We people-watched for a while and checked out some of the stores on the Plaza. Back on Fifth Avenue, we kept heading south until we reached the Empire State Building on Thirty-fourth Street.

"When was the last time you were up to the top?" Sharon asked.

"Not for a really long time. You want to go? The line isn't too long."

Unfortunately, the tickets were thirty-four dollars for the eighty-sixth floor main deck. We opted to just see the Art Deco lobby and continued on.

We were both hungry. A place called the Potbelly Café was nearby, and we stopped to fill up on some good sandwiches with a bag of cookies to go.

I was trying to remember the names of jazz clubs I had heard Drew talk about. We hailed a cab and asked the driver if he knew of the one on Eleventh Street. He said, "That's probably the Village Vanguard, but to get in you need to call to make a reservation. Smalls is on Tenth Street, and there's no entry fee there."

We called the Vanguard to make a reservation. There was a thirty dollar entry per person plus you pay for one drink. We thanked the driver with a good tip and waited outside for the eight-thirty set.

We were shown to our seats and ordered cokes from our server. The club patrons were very serious about respect for the performers and it wasn't surprising that there were no cell phone or talking interruptions during the set. When the band finished, we paid our check, and headed out.

Sharon said, "Should we start back home or try Smalls?" Since there was no cover charge, we decided to walk over. Sharon noticed that two college age guys started following us along the way to Tenth Street. There was a wait of a half hour there, but we were able to get seats for the ten thirty set. The place was so tiny we were right next to the bar. We showed our fake IDs, and this time ordered vodka and tonics. The quartet combination of organ, trumpet, guitar, and drum players put both of us in a great mood, but I couldn't shake the worry for my mom. We had been there for an hour and I was feeling restless. I said, "Why don't we head back to Grand Central."

We left our drinks behind and gave up our seats exactly when the two guys in back of us also got up. They introduced themselves as Sam and James. They seemed OK, and we talked to them for a few minutes. "Are you from the city?" Sam asked.

"We're on summer break but we'll be going back for our senior year in college in the fall," Sharon explained easily. "We're celebrating our twenty first birthdays together," she continued with a smile.

Sam said, "There's a couple of fun bars with music around here, why don't you two join us?" I saw Sharon looked very interested and I took about three seconds to think about it. Sam was decent looking, around five feet eleven, sandy brown hair and hazel eyes. His buddy James, was very cute, tall and curly dark hair, and not a jock.

We all decided it was a good idea as it was only eleven thirty. Sharon's mom had not called, which made it easier to stay for a little while longer. We paired off, Sam and I, James and Sharon.

"Where do you live?" I asked Sam as we entered the dance bar.

"I'm on Fourteenth Street off Fifth. Just a couple of blocks north of here."

"Are you working in the city?"

He replied, "Yes, I just started as a philanthropic advisor. You think of technology as being advanced now, but wait a little while. We help people get funding through corporate sponsors and find grants for the arts."

He asked about my plans for the future. I thought that being an art restorer for a museum would be a good career where you could learn the styles of Master artists, and that was my story.

For a Sunday night, there was a lively crowd inside, and a few people were dancing to a four-piece band performing '70s hits. Hey, we're in the city that never sleeps.

We stepped up to the bar pulling out our fake IDs again. Sam ordered vodka and tonics for Sharon and me while he and James took two beers to the table.

We watched the group for a few minutes until Sam said, "Let's get on that dance floor," pulling me up out of my chair. The two of us were singing with the crowd and ended up dancing in the middle of a circle of clapping people. Sharon and James got up and joined the fray as we pumped up the revelers. The band was great, and the place was jumping.

We cheered the band as they went on break and reluctantly returned to our table for a tall glass of water. We sipped our drinks for another twenty minutes while talking about things to see in the city.

It was time to get started back to the train station. I rose first and found my legs weren't cooperating. Sharon got up and nearly keeled over. We looked at each other confused. Things had just gotten out of control. I grabbed the table and tried to sit down, but knocked over the glasses. Sharon couldn't get out of her chair.

Both Sam and James shouted to the bartender, "Who was just over here?" pointing at our table. "Those vodkas were drugged." Two guys at the bar left quickly but we couldn't be sure they were the ones who spiked our drinks.

Sam said to James, "We need to stay with them for awhile. Make sure they're all right."

James said, "Get a taxi and we'll go to your apartment for some coffee."

Sam said to me, "Look, we're not deviants or trying anything funky. We'll take you to my place until you feel well enough to get home. We just want you safe."

I mumbled, "OK."

James went to hail a taxi and helped us in. The driver gave them a funny look, but James ignored it. The ride took only a few minutes to get to Fourteenth Street, but neither Sharon nor I could have walked there. Sam paid the driver and eased us out of the cab. We made it to the building door but needed help climbing the stairs to the second floor.

The entry hall led straight into the small living room with the kitchen and quartz island off to the right. Three doors on the left wall led to two bedrooms and one bath. I was never so happy to see a couch. Sharon collapsed into one of the leather chairs off the kitchen. James made coffee, but I was able to get only a few sips before falling asleep. Sharon was out before the coffee was even ready.

I woke up to a lot of yelling.

"The hell, Sam! What the ef are you doing with my sister here?"

"Your sister? That's your sister? Drew. Calm down. Wait. James and I brought them here to keep them safe. I don't drug girls, Drew. Someone else at the bar did it."

Drew said, "She's fourteen years old, man!"

"Whaddya mean fourteen? I saw her ID. She's twenty-one."

I opened my eyes and said, "Drew? How did you get here?"

"Phoebe, why are you even in New York?"

"Is there any more coffee, please? I can't think and speak right now."

More coffee was poured while Sharon was waking up. Once Drew got over the initial shock, he sat down.

"How do you know Sam?" I asked.

"Sam is my roommate. We were in the same dorm at Lehigh."

I looked over at Sharon. "What are the odds?"

I said, "Sam and James picked us up in a jazz club. Since when do you live in New York? I thought you were in Greenwich with Darleen."

"Mom kicked me out of the Greenwich house last month. Something about looking exactly like her 'ex-manwhore-swamp-leech-Charles'. I think she'd had a few at the time."

"Did she mean that Dad fooled around with other women?"

"Who knows? I called Sam, and his roommate had just gone out West. The room was available. Dad is spotting the rent until I'm employed."

"You and Sam hang out at cool places."

Drew said crossly, "You're fourteen, and you got into clubs and bars on your own? How much did you have to drink?"

"I can get around the city by myself. We had only one vodka in four hours. I wasn't drunk."

"So you lied to them about your age."

"Nope," I said. "I offered alternative facts."

At four in the morning our legs worked enough to go home. But the late hour meant that we missed the last train to Scarborough. We were in a pickle.

Drew had an interview Monday afternoon in Westchester, anyway, and he agreed to drive us back home. Thank goodness we wouldn't have to walk from Scarborough station at this time of the morning.

Sharon and I gave an awkward thanks and chaste kisses on the cheek to Sam and James.

"Goodbye, Phoebe. Goodbye, Sharon. Stay out of trouble," said James.

I'm sure they'd get a chuckle out of this sometime in the future.

We sat in the back seat of the Audi and stretched out for the trip home. Every time I looked over at Sharon, we were both smiling. A lot. What an excellent night!

When we turned into our driveway at four forty-five, I said to Drew, "You won't tell Dad. Right?"

Drew shook his head very slowly. "PS, I'll think about it."

One week ago, my life changed. Dad left. Mom needed help, but I, Phoebe Spring, managed to keep my head together with the help of my best friend and a family member I barely knew.

CHAPTER 5   WHAT TO BELIEVE

Drew was the one who woke Sharon and me after an hour and half of sleep. He must have stayed up all night.

"Coffee's on the kitchen table for the juvenile delinquents," he goaded.

I made toast for us, and thirty minutes later we went outside to wait for the school bus. It was going to be a really long Monday.

The last week of school was pretty much useless. There was one exam to take, but I'd been able to study before Mom's episode. Kids were playing lame jokes on each other and more or less had started summer break already. I was still staying with Sharon, so we had some free time to walk around the village and meet with friends after school.

At the deli we were talking to Asia, one of the cheerleaders, as we stood in line to place our order. "Uh, Phoebe, I think you might want to know about someone who's been sending you nasty texts."

I asked, "Do you know who? Do you know what the reason is? I didn't think I pissed off anyone this year. Except maybe the P.E. teacher."

"It's Jackie Lorrenze."

Sharon cut in, "I thought it was her voice. Do you know what it's about?"

"Are your parents friendly with hers?" Asia asked.

I answered, "Well, Mom and Barbara Lorrenze work together and are very good friends."

Asia warned, "Jackie's been talking about your mom and dad and what she's saying is cold. I thought you should know."

"Thanks for the heads-up, Asia. I definitely need to speak to her."

Sharon nodded, "She lives off Oak Road. You and I could walk over now and see her."

"No, it's getting too late today, Shar. I can take the bus to Jackie's house tomorrow after school and walk back to your house afterwards. It's only a couple of miles. I don't want to start anything with the girl. I just want to find out why she's calling me."

"I don't think you should go by yourself."

I had to be careful what I'd say to Jackie when I saw her. She must have known about Mom being in the hospital, but why she'd trash my father I couldn't figure out.

On Tuesday after school, Sharon and I left for Jackie's house. She wasn't on the bus, and we wondered if she would even be home. We walked up the driveway to the door. It looked like no one was there, but I knocked. I had just about given up when the door was opened by Barbara Lorrenze wearing a bathrobe.

"Uh, hi, Mrs. Lorrenze. Do you know anything about some calls I've gotten from Jackie?"

"Well, Phoebe. Uh…Jackie's, uh…Jackie lives with her father now…and I, uh, I'm not sure when…."

What I saw behind her is still embedded, engraved, carved, branded in my mind forever. There was my FATHER. In a bathrobe!

"Oh, nooooo! Jesus, Dad! What the…Why? What are you DOING here?"

Sharon was trying to steady me…. "Phoebe. Phoebe. Calm down, Phoebe." I was yelling at Dad and about to keel over on the walk.

I turned around and fled. Get away. Just run and get out of here.

I heard Dad calling, "Phoebe, wait."

Like I was going to talk to him while he's wearing a freakin' bathrobe. Sharon caught up to my panicked running, trying to talk me down from that awful sight. With a combination of fast walking, sprinting wildly, then stopping for a minute to scream out loud, Sharon stayed by me all the way to her house.

How could he have done this? What was he thinking? Jackie's mother, Barbara, was Mom's best friend, the ultimate catastrophe because he was sleeping with her. Now I understood the calls and texts.

I threw myself on the kitchen floor, sweaty, out of breath, dizzy and ready to throw up.

I yelled at Sharon, "No wonder he was driving nearby last week. He was going to see her. No wonder Jackie was leaving those messages on my phone. She knew all along about our parents' affair."

I was crushed. Mom would be devastated...unless she already knew. Maybe that was the final cut.

Sharon handed over a soda and sat on the floor opposite me.

"When was he out of town last?" She asked.

"Too many times to remember. Supposedly he was in New York." I was furious. I figured that Mom must have known at least something was going on, but maybe she wasn't aware of who he was with.

They used to be happy. Dad could charm the entire room and make everyone feel comfortable, while Mom was the organized one and managed the weekly schedule. We ate most dinners together, went on vacations together, laughed together. I thought we were a family. How could someone who had so much throw it all away? Is this how adults cope with getting older?

Something Drew said the other night became a beacon in my thoughts. Dad had done this before. He had obviously cheated on Drew's mother, judging from what Darleen said to Drew at her house in Connecticut. Then, Mom accused Drew of being the Devil. I realized that her state of mind was altered, but she knew Drew from the time he was eight years old. How could she think that?

Dad met Mom through Family Assistance. Mom was heading up their event committee and in walked Charles, a tall charismatic guy, with nearly black hair, brown eyes and effortless charm. He was immediately taken with Patrice's petite frame, blue eyes, blond hair and sophisticated manner. She was and still is, stunning. They were married six months later. That was how the story was told to me many times.

This was his third marriage. Mom's first. When they married, she was twenty years old. He was thirty.

Darleen was wife #1, who now calls him the "ex-manwhore-swamp-leech." No one ever talked about his second marriage that I can remember. I don't even know the name of #2. So if this were a pattern, maybe he cheated on wife #2 with my mom? I had to talk to Drew more about this.

At dinner, I asked Mrs. Sinks if she knew Barbara Lorrenze. "I was greeted at her door today with the two of them in matching bathrobes."

Mrs. Sinks didn't hold back her surprise. "I had no idea, and I'm so sorry that you found out like that," she said. "I told your father last week that I'm here if you want anything. And Phoebe, you know you can stay even after Sharon goes to her Grams if you wish."

"I don't know what to say. Thank you, Mrs. Sinks," I replied quietly.

Mrs. Sinks said that her real estate office had been extremely busy over the weekends and that they had listings of a few celebrities' properties for sale. She had shown a beautiful Tudor mansion a few times and presented an offer today.

I commented, "Most of my friends whose parents were divorced ended up in a downsized place. That could happen to me also."

Mrs. Sinks assuredly said, "After speaking with Charles, I understand that having to move would be a long way off, and you shouldn't worry about it."

Sharon and I stayed up for a long time and talked.

I asked her, "Do you think you and Irene will still be OK once she marries your dad?"

"It was going well pre-marriage, but anything can happen after it becomes permanent. Another thing is I don't like Irene's daughter much. I'd rather go places with just Dad 'cause Amy acts like a brat. She's twelve and talks back a lot, and I have to share her bedroom when I'm there. Awkward. I get to see Dad only a couple of weekends a month. He's so busy."

"But at least your mom and dad still talk to each other and can deal with any issues that come up," I countered. "I don't think that's ever going to happen with me again."

We watched reruns of *Downton Abbey* before lights out, but I was restless all night.

Wednesday started with a gorgeous morning. Sharon and I finished our last exam and last day and went to the pool. Oh, God, and there was Jackie. We were having fun and jumping in the water when I saw her drive up. She had just gotten a car, a red Chevy Cruze, I guess for her sixteenth birthday. I wondered if my Dad helped pay for it. The threesome walked into the pool area as Jackie pointed at me and they all started laughing. I couldn't believe it. The girl was relentless.

Sharon, noticing my clenched jaw and fists, stood in front of me to block the view. We ignored her, dried off and lay on the towels, but Jackie deliberately wandered over to our side talking just loud enough so that I could hear her say, "Stupid girl doesn't even know who her mother is." Her friends did not laugh at that, I noticed. I really wanted to pound her.

Mrs. Sinks picked us up later, dropped Sharon off first, then me at the house for an hour. I found the bank statements Dad needed, and as I pulled them out, I saw a folder labeled "Phoebe". I guessed that Mom would have saved everything about my life in there, but it was thin with only a few papers. I opened it up to find my birth certificate. A pink center with a blue border, Certificate of Birth from the City of New York.

Phoebe Anna Spring, plus my birthday at the top: July 21. And my Dad's name was on it. Father/Parent's Name: Charles W. Spring. When I saw what it read in the middle, dizziness blasted my head. Mother/Parent's Maiden Name: Keira M. Tierney. Keira? Have I ever heard that name before?

I sat down hard. I turned the paper over. Patrice Joy Ryan was nowhere on the certificate. I looked at the seal again. It looked official. I dropped the folder and took the paper to the copier. I looked at the copy as if the process would change the information and considered whom I would ask first about this. Why would they lie? Who was Keira Tierney?

Dad rarely mentioned his marriages. I looked at the paper again. I went to the computer and did a search for Keira M. Tierney. Nothing. I looked on Facebook. Nada. I was born in NYC. I went to Addresses on the computer. Nothing under that name in New York. Should I ask Mrs. Sinks? Maybe she would know who Keira was. This was not a time to sit back and wonder.

Still holding the copy, I brought it to the file drawer and noticed another unmarked folder tucked behind. I opened that up to find a hand written letter to Mom.

"Dear Patrice:

I've thought many times how you stepped in to take my little girl years ago. I know I had serious problems and was unable to care for her then. But at some point in the future, if she wants to find me, please let her know that I hope that one day, I can meet her.

Yours sincerely,

Keira Leighton

Stamford, Connecticut"

The date was from a year ago.

Now I had her married name. I went to my laptop and checked again with the new information. Her name appeared with a phone number. Mom had this information and chose not to share it. I wanted to scream.

"Drew, pick up, please, Drew!" I yelled into my phone. Voicemail. Mrs. Sinks would be back to get me in an hour. I paced the house. Walked outside for air. Then I had to sit down. They kept this from me all this time. My mother is not my mother!

I was visibly upset when Mrs. Sinks arrived. She looked at me as I got in the car. "What happened? Did you call your mom?"

I froze. "Who's my real mom?" I asked.

Mrs. Sinks gave me a squinty look. She didn't know what I was talking about.

When I walked into the Sinks' living room, I was trying to find the words to explain what my parents had been hiding from me. I was caught between anger and confusion until I finally broke down. Sharon asked, "What's the matter? You're shaking."

I choked out, "I just learned that Dad and Mom haven't been honest with me at all. Mom keeps insisting that I won't be there for her when she gets out. Now I understand why. It seems that everything I thought was real isn't."

Sharon tried waiting me out figuring I'd open up, but finally offered, "When my parents split up, it was so hard because I didn't want to take sides. They gave me a choice of who to live with. Like I could choose. I'm glad I stayed here, but I've really lost my dad. It's just not the same as before. I did get used to it, though. You will too, but it takes a long time."

Then everything got fuzzy. The combination of Keira, the breakdown, hate calls, the divorce, then camp, crushed my chest. I started wheezing and couldn't catch my breath. Sharon became alarmed and yelled to Mrs. Sinks. She rushed in and realized I was hyperventilating, grabbed a paper bag and said, "Breath in here." It took a little while until I felt OK.

I broke an awkward silence. "I think I'll go to bed now. Sorry I'm causing so much trouble."

Sharon caught up and tugged my sleeve. "I know you'll work through what's been happening. I'm here, you know."

My tummy was flipping over every time I remembered Keira's name—my birth mother. I wasn't going to be satisfied until I found out what happened to her.

Hoping for a fresh start Thursday morning, Sharon didn't hover or dwell on yesterday's events. My mute mood had not improved. Mrs. Sinks encouraged us to hang out in town to see friends. We brought a change of clothes with us to the pool and stretched out in silence.

We'd had a swim and around noontime, Thomas, a junior from Art Club, waved to Sharon and walked over. "Hey, Spring-fever, how's it going?"

"Yo," I answered.

"Where's your lady, Diana, Thomas?" Sharon asked, knowing I wasn't in a chatty mood.

He spread out his towel and sat. "Boo-hoo, hanky, please. The relationship flatlined yesterday."

"Well, sorry about that. You should drown your sorrows in massive quantities of cheese and tomato sauce. How about

69

pizza?" Sharon asked poking me. "C'mon, Phoebe, don't be a crab the last couple of days I'm here. We have to eat, anyway."

"Pizza's OK. I'm hungry," I said quietly. "Let's change first."

"I'm game," Thomas said. "Pizza Palace sound good?"

We took his VW convertible to my favorite pasta place. Most of the lunch crowd had left, so our large pie and sodas arrived quickly.

Thomas said, "I'm visiting my grandparents for a week in L.A. Mostly I'm lifeguarding at the pool. Are you two going to be around?"

Sharon took the last slice. "It's Philadelphia for me – to see Grams."

"My dad's sending me to Massachusetts for camp. I'll be back for the third week in August, though. Hopefully with a nice tan."

Just then, Jackie walked in with two friends and sat in the back. She gave me the finger. Twice in one week.

Sharon quickly spoke up, "Phoebes, just ignore her. You don't need any more stress."

I would have followed Sharon's very good advice had Jackie not stood up to her full five feet ten height and walked to our table shoving her finger in my face. "Your mom is whack, and your dad sucks. He's a low-class home wrecker, and you had no business going to my house, you bitch."

I was enraged. I gestured right back at her, "Stop with your stupid texts, and leave me and my family alone." I jumped up and connected my fist onto her jaw. The shock of slugging her, and the pain in my hand – wow that hurt – registered on my face. I caught my foot on the chair and fell backward onto Thomas, causing Jackie's return swing to miss.

"Whoa," Thomas shouted as he grabbed me when Jackie reached for my neck. She was going ballistic as Thomas and Sharon pulled us apart.

"Get out of here, all of you before I call the police," yelled Don, the owner.

We were bodily escorted out the door. Of course, Jackie wasn't finished, still yelling to me as I walked toward Thomas's car. "You're family is the dregs of this town! Why don't you just leave and make everyone happy?"

I was mortified for what I'd done. I've watched those reality judge TV shows enough to know I was in the wrong. No matter how provoked I was, I had put my hands on her first, and I could have caused so much grief for my parents, let alone being sued by a classmate for assault. Bad form, Phoebe, bad form.

I explained, "Sharon, I'm so sorry and Thomas, you too," as they caught up to me. "I can't believe I did that. That was so embarrassing," shaking my head.

Thomas said, "Actually, I thought it was kind of cool."

Sharon elbowed him. "What? Are you smirking?"

"I've never seen two girls fight before. Except on TV," he added. "What was that all about, anyway?" Thomas asked.

Sharon looked at me wondering if I would disclose the truth.

"There's a problem between our parents, Thomas. That's all I can say."

We climbed aboard his VW and took the long way back to Sharon's. He came in for a Gatorade and was up for a game of badminton, two against one. We ran around the backyard chasing a Frisbee to blow off bad energy until Mrs. Sinks pulled into the driveway. Thomas greeted Sharon's mom with, "Hey, Mrs. Sinks," as he started his car. "It was a memorable day, ladies," he winked. "See you in August."

Mrs. Sinks asked, "How was your first day of vacation?"

Sharon and I looked away and shrugged.

As soon as we went inside, I dialed the nurse's line at the hospital to get Mom. I waited a few minutes anxiously until she picked up. I was about to bring up the dreaded birth certificate, but Mom spoke first, "Oh, Phoebe. I'm sorry that you have to see me here. I just want to be home."

I almost hung up. No way could I bring up my birth mother now. If only Mom had trusted me. If only Dad had made her tell the truth. If only Mom hadn't gotten sick, or Dad hadn't hooked up with Barbara Lorrenze. Lies all around, each one a deeper stab into whoever's heart it touched.

"Mom, it will be OK. We just want you to be better. Are you able to take your medication? Have their been any problems with it?"

"I see Dr. Gordon every day. I am feeling better, Phoebe, I promise you I'll be home soon."

"I'll come back next week or if you need me sooner, Mom. I really miss you."

Mom sounded panicky, "You need to stay away from Barbara," Mom said a little louder. "She shouldn't be talking to you. Promise you won't go over there. All right? Promise."

"Uh, Mom. You don't have to worry. I'm definitely not going near her."

"No, I mean you'll want to leave. Just don't talk to her. Stay away from her. She'll try to tell you things that are wrong."

"Mom, please listen. I won't leave you. OK?"

"All right, Phoebe. I love you, don't forget."

"Me, too, Mom. I'll see you soon."

After that, I went upstairs to bed, fell asleep for an hour, then got up to join Sharon on the couch. We noshed on some celery and threw popcorn at each other in front of TV.

"Grams is expecting me on Monday," Sharon said. "I could probably stay with you a few more days before I leave."

"No, we still have the weekend together, and thanks, but I'll be OK. You're really lucky. Your Mom is great you know."

"Yeah. Yes, she is," Sharon said.

Long pause.

"I'm lucky, too. You're a good friend," I said.

"We sure had fun in New York. Yup. Wouldn't mind seeing James another time," Sharon said.

"Ha. In another six years you mean. Did you see the look on their faces when they found out our age?"

Sharon said, "When you get back from camp…"

Mrs. Sinks called us. "All right, girls, ready for dinner?"

"We'll set the table," we chimed.

CHAPTER 6   AVOIDANCE

On Friday morning, Mrs. Sinks picked us up in town to take Sharon home and me to my shrink. Dr. Landt invited me to sit and zeroed in on a relaxation technique she used.

She said, "First I want to show you how to regulate your breathing. Breathe in with your nose noticing how your tummy rises up as you take a good breath. Then exhale through your mouth pushing out with your abdomen."

I followed what she said. "If you try to practice this daily, it becomes easier. The next step is to think of a relaxing place that you enjoy and picture it clearly in your mind as you focus on your breathing." After a few more inhales and exhales, I opened my eyes.

"Now, what's going on with you?" she asked.

"I'm sure Mom knows who Dad's been seeing. Unfortunately, I do, too. I was at her house. She's Mom's best friend, and there's something else I just can't talk about. It's too painful."

"Oh, my. Let's take one thing at a time. Do you want to start with the best friend or your parents' separation?"

"I know my parents were arguing. I just didn't imagine that Dad would cheat with Mom's oldest friend. How could both of them hurt her so much? I know that Mom still loves Dad. She's totally screwed up over this. It could have been what caused the whole buying things she didn't need."

"Do you think that forgiveness is possible?"

"For what Dad did and what Barbara did? I doubt it."

"What if you learned that holding on to anger and disappointment can actually ruin your own life?"

I took a minute to think about what she just said.

"Mrs. Lorrenze's daughter, Jackie, is harassing me horribly with texts and phone messages. I think she painted 'Psycho Mom' on the side of our house. I couldn't take her yelling at me so I socked her in the jaw the other day. She blames my dad and my mom for breaking up her parents."

Dr. Landt said, "How do you think Jackie feels about her broken home?"

"I guess she's hurting. But I was mad at my dad, not at her – until she was threatening me."

"Everyone deals with disappointment and stress in different ways, Phoebe. If you practice your relaxation exercises, it'll help reduce your anger also."

I said, "Probably better than taking it out on someone else. I'll think about what you've said."

Early Saturday morning Drew drove in to pick me up for the hospital visit. Drew stayed in the car until it was time to meet with Dr. Gordon for a progress update.

Mom and I walked slowly around the halls as we chatted. I said, "Dr. Landt was helping me a lot with her breathing technique. Have you ever done that?"

"I did a long time ago," she said. "But now, the meds make me so sleepy, I would just doze off trying it, I think. I'm worried you won't want me home with you, Phoebe."

"That's not true, Mom. I'm here, and we'll work through this together. You'll get better, you'll see." She looked away. I said, "I'm going for my riding lesson this afternoon. When you come home, we should go together again like we used to. Wouldn't that be great?"

I was hoping that would perk her up, but she looked really sad. Too soon, I guess.

"You have to promise me you won't talk to Barbara."

"I already promised that. Why are you being so insistent about this? I have nothing to do with her."

"We were best friends, and I shared things with her. Don't believe whatever she says, Phoebe. Who'll be there for me if you leave?"

"I promise the person at home will be me. I promise, Mom."

After hugging her goodbye, she seemed less agitated, maybe from her meds, and I called Drew to meet me in Dr. Gordon's office for his update.

Dr. Gordon sat down opening a folder on his desk. He said, "Patrice's progress is not consistent yet, but the group and therapy sessions are going as well as expected at this stage. The specific bipolar medications will take a couple of weeks to regulate. Her depressed state has improved somewhat, although her highs are still a concern. She is interacting with the other patients which is a good sign. Patrice has also taken to writing letters about her observations here. She has shown several to me, and at some point I hope she shares them with you in particular, Phoebe."

I said, "She's worried about losing me. I keep saying I'm not leaving, but it keeps coming up. Has she said anything to you?"

"Your mother has mentioned a bad dream that you are angry at her and that you reject her."

After leaving the hospital, we stopped to get Sharon for our jumping lesson with Doris. Drew waited for us to change and gave us a ride to the barn. We had booked Waterboy and Postman and brought them out to the ring to warm up on the flat, while Doris set up the fences. Sharon did three verticals and the wall jump on Postman and then waited in the center for me to go. Waterboy did the three verticals, but at the wall stumbled forward thumping me into the wood base as I landed on my shoulder. Waterboy got up quickly but limped to the center where Doris caught the reins and made him stop.

She yelled, "Phoebe, are you all right?"

I stayed there for a second to be sure nothing was broken. Sharon rushed over as I said, "I think so. No damage. Just banged up."

I rubbed my sore spot while walking back to Waterboy, worried about his leg.

Doris said, "He may have pulled something. I'll get the liniment. How do you feel, Phoebe? Do you want to continue with the lesson on Quincy?"

"I'm fine, just a stiff shoulder. I'll get Quincy ready now."

I warmed him up on the flat while Sharon took some more fences. When it was my turn, we did the three verticals with just the wall jump left to do. Quincy did the three strides toward it but dove to the right flinging me off balance to the left. Doris called out, "Do your circle and come right back to it."

I concentrated on the center of the wall, and together we went over.

"Now come around and do it again."

We circled, did three strides, and Quincy balked to the right. I knew it was my fault and not Quincy's.

"Come to the center."

"Phoebe, Quincy has done that wall a hundred times. You are not communicating where you want to go. Stop for today, and walk him out, but the next time, there's no reason for you to be avoiding the walls. Next lesson, tell yourself you'll do better."

I was so disappointed I messed up. Sharon said, "Look, everyone has a bad day. You just weren't together. It'll be fine."

I called Drew when we were done. He did a double take looking at the slight bruise on my cheek as I got in the car. We dropped off Sharon and made plans for lunch the next day, Drew's treat.

Drew asked, "What's wrong, Phoebes?"

"I was looking forward to my lesson, and I screwed it up – fell on my face once and almost twice more."

After taking Sharon home, he offered, "Hey, you know by now things don't always go the way you plan. I know it sucks. I'm surprised you can concentrate on anything with what's going on with your mom."

"Yeah. It sucks," I said. "How's your job plan going?"

He did that pouty thing with his mouth and said, "It sucks."

Drew could make a mugging victim laugh off the experience.

On Sunday, Drew came through on his lunch promise for the three of us. Sharon and I polished off dessert while looking at the Hudson River from my favorite Ossining restaurant. I planned to tell Drew first about my birth mother, but the timing was always off.

The coffee arrived and Drew said, "Dad spoke with the camp director, Mrs. Finnegan, and you're all set for the equestrian program. We'll leave next Friday morning around ten for Massachusetts. It's pretty close to Tanglewood, so we have tickets for the concert Friday night."

I jumped, "Are you kidding me? That's fantastic! Oh, my God! Is this to make up for telling Dad about our city trip?"

Drew was caught. "Maybe I felt a little guilty."

Sharon punched me in the arm. "Oh, man, wish I could go too."

Drew continued, "We stay Friday night at the Hampton Inn and head for camp Saturday morning."

"I am so jealous," Sharon said.

I pointed out, "You know, Dad has time to make all these plans but can't spend three minutes speaking to me. He's throwing money at this mess and hoping I'd forget about where Mom is."

Drew answered, "Look, don't you think Dad is having trouble facing these problems, too? He probably wishes he could take a break from the stress. I'm sure he'll call you when you get there. The camp allows you to check your phone for messages, so we'll keep you up to date on Patrice. You can write letters instead of texting."

"Writing a letter? I guess I'll need stationery," I said.

Drew dropped us at Sharon's, and we spent the rest of Sunday evening packing her clothes for her trip to Phily. Sharon had some paperbacks to read on the train, and on Monday morning, I helped my best friend carry her bags out to the car.

Mrs. Sinks said, "Quickly, girls, the train won't wait for us."

Sharon said, "Don't be upset," when she saw I was crying. "I'll see you in a couple of weeks."

"Too much has happened. I'm sad to see you go," I said.

"But you're going to have a great time riding the whole summer while I'm back here waiting for you to get your ass home. Just don't forget to call me – like every day, you jerk."

I made a face. "We'll talk then."

"And stay out of trouble, remember?" She gave me that we've-got-a-secret-look, and I laughed. They left for the train station for Sharon's two-hour Amtrak ride to Philadelphia.

CHAPTER 7   WHO'S TO BLAME

I was alone for the first time since Mom went to the hospital. I called Dad. Voicemail, of course. I left a message to call me back; I had the paperwork he wanted. Every time I thought about the birth certificate, Keira's letter, and what I'd say to Dad, my stomach flipped over. He was the one I had to confront. Having a blow up at Mom wouldn't accomplish anything, no matter how anxious I felt about it.

If I could take some sketches to the hospital on Tuesday, maybe that would distract her, and let me think about something else. I looked over the drawings I'd done in the last week including the fox Sharon and I saw on the trails. That was OK, but then a pasture idea came to my mind. I took a new sheet and drew a girl standing in a meadow with her horse. I added a rustic post-and-rail fence with a copse of shade trees behind her, plus a long stone wall in the distance. The last drawing ended up as a Maple Hill barn with a girl leading a horse out to the ring. I placed the studies in a small portfolio to carry with me.

Tuesday morning Mrs. Sinks and I went to the hospital. We were shown to Dr. Gordon's office first for another update. He reported that group therapy was not productive and that they decided to focus on private sessions for her.

Dr. Gordon said, "Her confusion with what is real or fantasy has not been resolved, so individual meetings are continuing as we had discussed last week. I think with future sessions, her erratic behavior will diminish. The imagined events are still troublesome, especially concerning the dreams that Phoebe leaves her. She believes that Charles and another woman are conspiring to take Phoebe away. The therapy is focusing away from her fears and concentrating instead on her commitment to her home and work responsibilities. This process will take some time."

As we neared the community area, Mom brightened up for a second when she saw Mrs. Sinks. However, she confused her with Barbara Lorrenze and became upset.

"Uh, wait, Mom, you remember Ellen Sinks." She sorted out her mistake while I thought of some good memories we had at the beach together, and of our riding at Maple Hill. I said, "We'll go riding together when you come home, right, Mom? I know the perfect horse for you, too."

Mom replied, "I used to ride Alfie, but I doubt he's still there. He was a wonderful hunter. I was reading a story the other day about the Rockefeller Park in *New York Magazine*. I did love to ride on the trails before you were born."

I said, " Mom, Alfie was still there when I first started. What else do you remember from Maple Hill?"

"Oh, I loved exploring the trails. I never actually got lost, but sometimes it would be a round-about way getting back to the barn with an excuse why I was so late."

"It's nice to have good memories, isn't it?" I asked.

"But the bad ones keep coming back. I can't stand it that I'm here, and I can't protect you from her," I could see Mom getting anxious.

Uh, oh. She's bringing up Barbara again. "No, Mom, you don't have to worry. Anyway, I told you I'm going to be at camp starting next week. And I can call you every week."

Mrs. Sinks added, "Phoebe's been a wonderful guest, Patrice. She's so helpful. Everyday she's thinking about something to make for you...like the sketches she brought today."

I pulled out the drawings from the folder. She studied each one and said, "This is like the field at the top of the hill. I remember that and the little fox. It's perfect. I'd like to keep these."

We got up to leave, and Mom stood to hug me. She looked so tired.

85

We went to the Sinks' house and fixed sandwiches before Mrs. Sinks went on to her next appointment. Dad finally called. "Sorry, Phoebe, I had back-to-back meetings and just took a break. How about I come by around five thirty tonight?"

My stomach was doing a million flips. "OK, but you need to bring me back to our house for the papers."

He asked, "How did your mom do today? Oh, sorry Honey, I've got another client meeting now."

"I'll tell you about it later. Bye, Dad."

"Sorry again, I'll see you tonight."

Dad drove up to the Sinks' at six. I wanted to talk to him privately, and we drove back to our house. He poured some water and sat down at the kitchen table while I found the documents. I placed the bank information and the birth certificate in front of him. He was focused on Mom's account and had not seen the other.

He glanced at the second one and his expression went sour.

He looked at the paper, not at me. "Where did you get this?"

"Where is she, Dad? Where is Keira Tierney, my mother?" That's when I broke down crying.

Dad was out of his seat quickly taking my arms. "Did your mother tell you about this?"

I looked up through tears, "I found that when I looked for the bank statement." I was crying and couldn't stop. "Why has everyone lied?"

He looked toward me for a long time, waiting for me to be in control. I grabbed some tissues, and blew my nose, and started on another round.

Finally, he said, "Please know that I've wanted to tell you since the time you were very little. This has been nagging at me, and I knew you'd have to find out. You'd need that birth certificate for getting your driver's license next year. It was a difficult situation with the wrong timing."

"Why didn't you tell me?" I said loudly.

"You know that I was married to Drew's mother, Darleen. You also know that we divorced. I married again very shortly after that to the woman on that paper, Keira Tierney. She was a struggling actress in New York, and I met her at an off-Broadway show. We married several months later, but what I didn't know was that she had an uncontrollable gambling habit. When she was supposed to be going to auditions, she was going to Atlantic City. She wiped out our finances, and we could barely pay rent. I then found out that she was pregnant with you. That's the only positive result from that marriage."

"But if she were my real mother, what was such a big deal? Then I'd know who I was."

"No, Phoebe. You're you because of who raised you. Because of Patrice, who is much more your real mother than Keira Tierney ever could be," he said.

I reached for a new tissue. "I just don't understand why you didn't say anything. I'm the last to find out about my own birth mother, and your fooling around with MOM'S BEST FRIEND. How could you do that?" I jumped up. "Dad. Why would Jackie Lorrenze know about this?"

"What?"

I said angrily, "She was at the pool. She said something like, doesn't even know who her mother is. What was that about?"

"I have no ide---," he looked like someone had smacked him. "Oh, my God." He got up and looked around, grabbed his keys and said, "I'll be back. Please don't leave. OK, Phoebe?"

I said, "Wait, where are you going?"

He slammed the door and I could hear the car roar out of the driveway. What else could go wrong?

Drew called me two minutes later. He was coming to see Dad about his job interview. "Are you staying at the house tonight?" he asked.

"I'm not sure. Dad left after we had a big argument. Mrs. Sinks is expecting me now, but I'll call her and stay here for you."

I waited for one of them to show up. Drew arrived first. He took a beer out of a cooler he brought and sat in the living room with me. "So what's going on?" he asked.

As he sat there with his feet up on the coffee table, I became crazed. First, he looked exactly like Dad, and second, he knew who his mother was. I had to remind myself that Drew was the one who stepped up to help more than anyone else.

"Patrice Spring is not my real mother."

He was in the middle of a pull on his beer and choked. "Phoebe, what the hell are you talking about?"

I walked into the kitchen and picked up the certificate and thrust it on his lap. "That is what I found earlier in a folder marked Phoebe."

He put the beer down and looked it over. "Holy shit."

"Exactly. At least I wasn't the only one who didn't know. Everyone else seems to have."

"Do you want to talk about it?" he asked.

"I still don't know everything. If Dad ever gets back here I want to find out if he knows where she is, who she is, what's happened to her," I said.

Silence.

"Can you stay here with me, please?" I asked quietly.

"Of course I will," Drew nodded.

We sat at the kitchen table, and I peppered him with questions.

"Do you remember meeting Keira?" I asked.

"Phoebe, I was like six when Mom and Dad split up. I lived in Greenwich. When he first left, I didn't see much of him then 'cause my mom was really angry. That I remember."

"So, he must have been fooling around with Keira behind your mom's back."

"If he married Keira so soon after the divorce as you said, I would imagine so."

"And he's done it again," I sighed.

"Shit happens," Drew pouted.

"Don't be like Dad, OK?"

Drew and I had just finished a dinner of eggs and toast when Dad came in around nine. He took a beer from Drew's cooler. We sat down together.

"I am so sorry about this, and I know my being sorry won't make you feel better because the truth is, I'm to blame, and that's not easy to accept. But there were many reasons for this happening and you should know. Your mom and I were married six months after my divorce from Keira. Patrice wanted a child so badly right away, but after a year, we went to a doctor only to learn that she would never be able to carry a child full term. During this time, I had gotten a very good job and was still supporting Keira and you, but she was still gambling. I was told that she was leaving you at home alone and not caring for you properly. I could not tolerate it, got an attorney, fought for full custody, and won. She did not fight it. The addiction took over her life, and nothing could stop it then.

"Patrice was in awe of you immediately. From the first moment she picked you up, she was in love. You became her focus and reason for living, and I was so happy that she finally was able to have a child even though it wasn't one she gave birth to."

I was crying and couldn't stop. I said, "How can a mother abandon her only child. Who does that? How could I have been so terrible that Keira would just reject me?"

"That's addiction. Gambling for some people is irresistible and almost impossible to beat. It's what happened later with your mom that led to all this. I wanted to tell you, and repeatedly brought this up to Patrice when you were much younger, but I could see that she convinced herself that Keira would come back to take you away. She would become hysterical about it. I finally gave up trying to make her tell you. I should have insisted, but I was on eggshells with her anxiety."

"How old was I when you won in court?"

"You were a year and a half."

He stopped talking. I still couldn't accept that as the whole story and wanted all of it, but Dad said, "If you have more questions, I'll answer them but not right now. I need to go back to the city for tomorrow's meeting."

"Who else knew, Dad?" I asked as he got up.

Dad looked at me for a long time. I could tell he was upset...no, angry, at the question. "Barbara Lorrenze. I believe she was the only one your mother confided in other than our doctors who knew about Keira giving you up."

I burst into tears again and ran out of the kitchen and upstairs to my room slamming the door as hard as I could.

I lay on the bed sobbing my guts out. The cruelest truth of all – Barbara Lorrenze and now Jackie Lorrenze had wormed their way into my most private moments and knew about all of this, and Dad chose her over Mom.

Dad knocked on the door. "Phoebe, I'm so sorry it happened this way. I promise to make this better."

"I don't see how now. Mom will be destroyed. She was devastated before, but now you've jammed a knife into her heart...and mine. She doesn't even know how I found out yet."

He opened the door. He said softly, "Phoebe, you are forgetting who took care of you, thought of you as her own child, and would do anything to protect you. You have two parents who love you more than anything else. You are correct that you should have been told by now. You were not because of the reasons I have said. Even though I've made mistakes I will never apologize for saving you from a horrific life with my ex-wife."

I listened and knew that Dad was correct. The shock was still raw, but his words were true. He sat down on the bed. "I love you, Phoebe and that is all that matters. No one is going to take you away from your mother and me."

I stopped crying. Dad left and Drew stayed. We didn't even get to talk about his interview. Drew said no matter, he'd catch Dad at the office the next day.

I said, "Will you call me later to tell me if you get an offer? I'd like to know if you'll be happy with it."

Drew said, "Of course, Phoebes. I'll want to know that you're doing OK, too."

After Drew left for New York on Wednesday afternoon I called Mrs. Sinks to ask if I could stay with her until Friday. Drew had an interview, but he'd be back for our trip to Massachusetts. I finished packing the trunk for the summer with riding gear, tops, shorts and books.

I was still hurting, but Dad didn't care enough to call me. I should call Keira myself. They kept the secret all this time. I sat staring at the birth certificate. I grabbed my pen, looked up Keira Leighton's Connecticut number on my laptop, and wrote it down. I paced around the house for an hour figuring out what I'd say. Keep it simple if it's voicemail. Don't be angry. Be calm. Heart pounding. Stomach flipping. What if she answers?

I called her number. Voicemail.

My heart was still thumping heavily as I said, "This is Phoebe Spring calling. I'd like to speak with Keira Leighton." I left my cell number.

Mrs. Sinks was in an all-day real estate class leaving me no way to see Dr. Landt, but with Drew's help, maybe I could come back from camp in a couple of weeks for a session.

I must have checked my phone a dozen times to see if there was a message – nothing.

Drew arrived Friday morning at the Sinks' at ten. I gave Mrs. Sinks a hug as Drew and I were leaving, and I told her how much I appreciated everything. We had to stop at my house to load the car but were on the road by 10.

I left a note and drawing for Mrs. Sinks and Sharon at my house.

"Dear Mrs. Sinks and Sharon,

Your friendship means so much. It was very kind of you to let me stay these past two weeks. I'm very grateful, and thank you for helping Mom and me.

Love, Phoebe"

I texted Dad to please send it on to her.

After a late lunch we drove to Tanglewood Music Center in Lenox, Massachusetts.

"Oh, my gosh, Drew. Look at this huge crowd," I remarked.

Many people were relaxing on the meadow that surrounded the Shed, the open-air structure where various bands and the Boston Symphony Orchestra perform.

Drew pointed to where we'd be sitting. "Dad got us center stage seats up ahead."

When the band started, the melodies shoved aside my anxiety for the evening. It was loud and comforting to hear all my favorite tunes. Drew yelled in my ear over the music volume, "I hope this is the beginning of a good summer for you, Phoebe."

"Thanks for sharing it with me!" I yelled back.

The hit tunes plus a few I hadn't heard before came to an end too soon.

When we arrived at the inn later than expected, there was a mix-up in the number of rooms reserved. I said it was fine to share as long as there were separate beds. Drew chuckled and carried the bags upstairs.

I had so many unanswered questions about Dad's life before me. "What was it like living without Dad when you grew up?" I asked.

Drew sat in a chair by the window. "He was around more than you think. I remember him coming to a lot of my sports events all through high school. Mom was so bitter about their divorce, like I said, he stopped seeing me for about a year. Later, though, I did see him on the weekends pretty regularly."

I pushed on, "Didn't you get mad at him for leaving?"

"Well, I was only six at the time, remember. So I didn't have a say about it. What was upsetting was my mom's constant criticism of him. He left her for someone else, and she never let anyone forget it."

"So, you didn't see him with Keira?"

"No. He wasn't married to her that long."

"And you don't know exactly when he met Mom."

"I wasn't at their wedding, but you remember I was at your house for holidays. You were a pretty cute kid."

"Yeah. You gave me my first horse sculpture after the *Black Stallion* movie. I must have watched that video a hundred times."

"Then your mom and dad got you started with riding lessons."

"Why did they lie to me, Drew?"

"There had to have been a really good reason, and Dad did try to explain it. I can't imagine how you feel about Keira."

"I just want to know why, I guess. Why wasn't I good enough?"

"That's the wrong direction. It's why SHE wasn't a good enough person to take care of you. Understand the difference?"

"I guess. I always wondered why I didn't look more like Dad or Mom. You're like a mirror image of him. Now I wonder what Keira looks like…if I have her height or color hair, or artistic talent. I need to know." I left out the part that I already tried to call her.

"When the right time comes, I think you'll get your answers."

As I turned down the bed covers, I was remembering how everyone must have difficult experiences, but at least I had people to lean on. What would have happened if Mrs. Sinks hadn't been available for these past few weeks, or Drew hadn't found me in New York, or I didn't have a best friend? Would I have done more stupid things?

Right after breakfast we started for the camp. Drew zipped us through back roads and hills offering pretty views of lakes and distant mountains. A long driveway decorated with balloons and a big "Welcome To Camp Thistle Creek" sign led to the camp. A large peak-roofed building was next to a parking area and a couple of smaller cabins. We followed the sign pointing to the entry to the main dining hall/auditorium. Younger kids were being organized into groups, while their parents were gathered in the reception section. The older kids were over by a jukebox speaking with a couple of counselors.

I asked, "Can you hang out a few minutes while I check out the instructions for the day?"

"I'll wait over here with the hot moms," he replied. I poked him in the ribs.

Two of the girls greeted me as I joined the circle and introduced themselves as Pam and Jane. The counselors asked everyone to take a seat for orientation and assignments to our cabins.

About five minutes later, we were welcomed by the Camp Director, Mrs. Finnegan, who from the stage, introduced the staff, outlined rules, distributed the schedule for our first day, and excused us to go with our counselors.

I went back to Drew and dropped my eyes. I was kind of looking forward to being here for the summer, so I didn't think it would be so hard to say goodbye. He barely knew me, was not responsible for my safe-keeping, and yet he was there in a way nobody else could be. Again, I wondered how the summer would have turned out had he not come forward to help.

I gave him a huge hug and said, "Thanks for everything, Drew. Um, you've been great to me. I hope I didn't wreck any of your plans these past couple of weeks."

Drew responded, "Just stay out of trouble, Phoebes. You can write or text to let me know how you are, OK? If Patrice wants to see me before I go back to the city, I'll stop at the hospital."

I yelled as he walked back to his car, "When I get back home, I want that driving lesson!"

CHAPTER 8   EIGHT LITTLE INDIANS

I caught up to our head counselor, Brianna Tempe, who was taking the oldest girls ages fifteen and sixteen, to Seneca, our cabin. She called out loudly, "Thistle Creek repeat campers, Robin Fisk and Alicia Adler?"

The two answered, "Here we are!"

Brianna responded, "Lead the way, ladies!"

We followed them to the end of the lane. I found Seneca to be pretty spacious for eight girls, with three of us from New York. There were two bunks against the wall, but I chose one of the four singles as Robin put her duffle on the bed next to mine.

Brianna called the Seneca and Iroquois girls to gather for the camp tour.

I pointed to a wide path that cut in between the woods and asked Brianna, "Where does that trail go?"

She said, "To the riding area and barn. Follow me – we'll see that first," as she trekked up the hill.

The path connected to a dirt driveway at the top that took us past a fenced paddock with four horses. Up ahead, a good-sized barn with eighteen stalls faced another structure with an open side for farm vehicles and a truck. The barn was very clean with a tack room and office off to the right. I took in the familiar smell of oats and horses that barns have and wished our lessons started that day.

Robin asked, "Are you signed up? I took riding last year here. It's a terrific program."

I noticed the sand ring and a fenced-in grassy meadow with various jumps set up. "Yes, my dad arranged everything. I'm supposed to be in the equestrian group. Can't wait to start."

We walked toward the spring-fed pond and passed a blue and white RV parked near the front paddock.

Brianna remarked, "The riding program is five days a week. It'll start on Monday with an evaluation of your riding skills by Mrs. Tully, the director."

That's when I found out that the two other girls from New York had riding experience and were also in the same program as me.

We backtracked down the hill, on toward the other cabins, the nurse's office, the bathhouse, and the Arts and Crafts Studio. The pool was on the main lawn near the flagpole across from the dining hall and parking area. Beyond that were the tennis courts on an adjoining property belonging to the owner of the camp.

Back at the main hall, we ate lunch with the counselors who answered questions on the daily schedule. First bell was at eight with breakfast at eight thirty. The riders could be scheduled for the morning or afternoon session. For the other activities, I decided to sign up for tennis, swimming and art and wondered if I should try archery, placing that on the maybe list.

There was free time Saturday afternoon to go to the crafts building, so I decided that would be a good place to start. Robin and Pam Lerner from Seneca, had already arrived, and I took a seat next to them. What a pair those two made. Robin's gorgeous fair complexion, long silky blond hair, and five feet seven height was the exact opposite of me. Pam Lerner was also tall with the most beautiful red hair falling to the middle of her back. We laughed while finishing ridiculous portraits of each other.

Pam said, "Oops, I forgot to add my freckles," and dotted her face with green and red markers.

Robin said, "Oh, my gosh. That looks just like the control-freak boyfriend I left back home. Actually, that's why I'm sitting here today. I couldn't wait to get here. He was making my life a living hell."

The face I drew was half horse, half man, and I called it "the man-hor". We all got a laugh out of that one.

Robin, Pam and I walked over to the main hall for dinner, finding our assigned table by the front windows.

"Let's make this a great summer," Robin toasted as we clinked our water glasses for good luck. The meal arrived, and everything was tasty, but I'd definitely ask Dad to send a care package with some good snack items.

I was chatting with Chantel Hunter, a pretty, soft-spoken African-American girl as we left the dining hall. I asked her, "When you aren't at school, what do you like to do?"

She responded, "I'm an entertainer at heart, and I bet I can get everybody here pumped up in the next five minutes."

Chantel was true to her word, inspiring most of the fifty campers to follow her dance and song routine to *Boom Chicka Boom*, on the way back to our cabins.

When we reached Seneca, Alicia yelled, "That was awesome, Chantel! Do you know the words for *Roar?*"

Chantel pulled her guitar from her bunk and amazed us with her voice and memory for pop tunes while we sat on the floor singing along with her.

Even with this group of nice girls, the thought of Mom locked in a hospital room was haunting. I tried to join in the fun but feared my camp adventure could end up being a bitter experience.

I was checking my phone every day, but still no message was returned from Keira. Every Sunday morning the camp slept late with breakfast at nine followed by church, which was located just a short walk away, or reading time. We could choose to join the different activities of archery, softball, swimming, or tennis, as well as ping pong or cards. When the girls cleared out, I pulled out my phone and decided I would try again to contact Keira. The anticipation of speaking with her was killing me. Wasn't she even curious to return the call I made a week ago? I wasn't giving up now. I pressed her number and hit Send.

"Hello?" a girl answered as my stomach flew up into my throat.

"My name is Phoebe Spring. May I speak with Keira, please?" My hands were shaking.

"She's not here right now. I can take a message."

I gave her my name and number and hung up. Damn. Hell's bells. Back to square one. This was much harder than I thought it would be.

Back at the cabin after dinner I was able to put Keira out of my mind when the girls started talking about the past school year.

Jane Bradley perked up. She was my height, with pretty hazel eyes, shoulder length curly brown hair, and turned out to be the most unpredictable of all of us. "I used to sneak out with my boyfriend, Todd, on school nights. I slipped and fell off the lowest end of the roof and broke my ankle. With all the racket going on Dad came running outside, and Todd took off. I ended up in the emergency room. That's when my father had enough, so I'm here and not with Todd, the troublemaker. They're hoping I'll forget about him while I'm gone."

Jane's story gave Pam an idea. "Everyone sit in a circle here," she motioned to the floor around her. "Tell something that happened to you that you would not wish on somebody else."

We looked at each other and gathered around.

Chantel offered, "I'll go. I was shopping in this nice store in Boston, and my gauzy skirt got caught in the elevator door. I walked away and a big section tore off the back leaving my pink-thonged booty on full display until a sales girl caught up with me."

Jane said laughing, "At least you've got a nice butt!"

Chantel looked over her shoulder seductively, "That's not the first time I've heard that."

Pam said, "I had a crush on a guy at school, and I sent him a text, but I pressed the wrong address, and it went to some girl. It spread all over school I was the gay chick for awhile." Groans followed that one.

Alicia volunteered, "I had this really cute stretchy bathing suit I'd just gotten, and there was no mirror in the bathhouse. I put it on in a big rush, and I got the bra on backwards. Anyway, the top fell down as I walked onto the beach. Then I saw my boobs had popped out to say hello." A collective "Woo-Hoo" sounded.

I groaned, "There were eight of us on a quadruple date. The usher at the play was showing where our seats were, but I cut him off and said, 'I think we can find it from here.' Then I caught my heel on the carpet and rolled down about twenty stairs with my skirt up to my crotch."

Linda Bonner said quietly, "I fell asleep sitting in class and started to drool a little. Someone took a video and posted it on youtube. It went viral."

Sandy Zimmerman told us, "I went to my brother's wedding last month and sneaked all the champagne I could find. I got really tired and passed out on one of the guest room beds upstairs. I woke up and the maid of honor was sound asleep with her arm draped over me."

"Whoooa," came from everybody.

Pam said, "Just before I left for camp, my Dad was teaching me how to park the Jeep. I got distracted when I saw this cute guy I liked walking by, and I backed into a police car. When he came up to the window, I was too embarrassed to roll it down."

Chantel announced, "OK, now we know everyone's worst nightmare. Mom packed me some chocolates. Anybody want some?"

We all jumped on her bed and dove into her Russell Stover box.

CHAPTER 9 LESSONS LEARNED

Monday started with a bell, loud and clear at eight. We dressed and headed for the bathhouse to wash up and continued to the dining hall. After we were seated according to cabins, the morning announcements were made followed by a big breakfast.

Robin, Pam, Jane and I changed into boots, britches and grabbed helmets. I was enjoying the great hair day, no humidity, as we headed up the hill to the barn. Mrs. Tully was checking out one of the horses. I figured she was in her forties, about five feet five, very solid and strong. You could tell she worked out a lot. Her brown hair had been bleached by the sun and pulled back into a short ponytail. She had those steely blue eyes that can sum up a person in a minute.

She remarked, "I understand that you four have requested equitation, so let's start with your barn sense."

While standing in the aisle between the stalls, Mrs. Tully indicated which horse each of us was to place on the cross ties. She watched as we brushed them out and cleaned their hooves. Mrs. Tully then pointed to the tack room and helped us find saddles and bridles. She checked girths and saddles and led the way to the ring where we mounted up.

We were directed in a walk, posting and sitting trot, and canter with change of leads and direction. After twenty minutes, she was satisfied that the four of us were around the same level and opened the gate to the meadow where the jumps were set up.

Mrs. Tully asked Pam to try the two feet six inch cross rails in the center of the paddock as we followed. We cantered around twice along the fence and jumped one vertical, then two more, and slowed to a walk. The same course was done again with an added vertical set at two feet nine inches. We continued walking quietly until Mrs. Tully flagged us back to the barn to water the horses.

She said, "You four will be in the same group. Be on time tomorrow morning. I'll have you signed up for two activity sessions starting at ten."

We thanked her as we un-tacked the horses, brushed them, and put them back in the stalls.

As we were leaving, an older guy dressed in blue jeans and work shirt came over.

"I saw you riding earlier. Looks like you've done it before. I'm Frank, the groom for the barn."

He was short but stocky with tan-lined skin, and I figured him to be in his early fifties. His cropped gray-brown hair sported a well-worn Red Sox baseball cap shading two flinty blue eyes.

"Hi. This is Pam, Robin, Jane, and I'm Phoebe. Is that your camper in the back? I saw it yesterday on the tour," I said.

"That's my place. Jean likes having someone on the grounds at night. Around here, we occasionally get critters getting too nosy. I have to run them off."

"Critters? Like bears?" Jane asked.

"No, mostly coyotes or foxes. They go after the barn cats."

"Well, nice to meet you, but I guess we have to get going."

We needed to change our clothes at the cabin to go for a swim. On the way we met two other Seneca girls just coming back from their activity.

"What did you and Alicia do this morning?" Jane asked Chantel.

"We went to archery and then to doubles tennis. Alicia and I were on competing teams, so that was fun. She's got a wicked backhand. How was your ride?" Chantel asked.

"We were just assessed today. Mrs. Tully said that the four of us'll be in the same group. I think you go for the first time tomorrow afternoon?" I asked her.

"Yes. But I heard Mrs. Tully is pretty strict with her crew." Chantel remarked.

"I guess she has to be if she's responsible for the horses and the barn," countered Pam. "But she knows what she's doing. You're going to love riding."

The girls had some down time at the cabin, and I took pen and paper to write to Drew.

"Dear Drew,

If you can't find a job this summer, you, Sam, and James should open a jazz club in Maple Ridge at the old vacant firehouse. Sharon and I will be happy to be your bouncers and check out all your college buddies. The camp is great. Thanks for the push to make me come here. Please come visit when you get a chance.

Love, PS"

"We're going to the pool for a quick swim before lunch. You wanna come with?" Robin asked.

Alicia said, "Oooh, maybe we'll see Andrew Finnegan there. He's the owner's son. He was kind of geeky last year, but, wow, he got really cute, and he has a friend."

We were able to get in a few laps before lunchtime. When we were playing chicken in the pool, I decided I'd write to Mom and send her the layout of the place when we got back to Seneca. I remembered that her parents had sent her to a riding camp when she was about my age. Maybe the things happening here could jog some good memories for her.

Lunch was a buffet with a sandwich and salad set up. I selected a turkey combo with salad on the side, then angled my way to our Seneca table at the back of the room by the big windows.

Robin said, "Last summer, the Iroquois girls had just finished their water ballet when one of the parents drove her convertible into the swimming pool."

Alicia added, "And the tennis instructor ended up being arrested for bank robbery. Doubtful the camp would share that on their website."

There was a lot of kidding back and forth, but Linda was the only girl who displayed a nasty streak. She had short dark hair and always wore long sleeves. I made a mental note to remember my first impression of her when she had said some negative comments over the past week. This time, after listening to her single out a girl from the Iroquois cabin saying, "Oh, God, look at the dorky print on those cropped pants she's wearing. Is this a clown school?"

I replied, "Wow, Linda, that was harsh. If you talk like that about everybody when they're out of earshot, you'll be sitting by yourself for the rest of the summer," and stood up to leave the table.

The girls went silent, and Linda looked mortified. I didn't care – I was so disgusted. What is the purpose of belittling someone for the sake of getting attention anyway?

Robin said, "Wait for me, Phoebe," As she got up at the same time. Pam, Chantel, and Jane followed, clearing their places, leaving Linda stewing in her seat. Maybe the girl would get the hint.

On our way back to Seneca, Robin raised her eyebrows and spoke in a low voice. "I'll tell you something fun we can do if you're up for it," she said, smiling. "The meals are great here, but sometimes I just want some junk food and stuff. You know, like chocolate kisses and trashy magazines. There's a country store about three miles away. Last year, I cut out during one of the activities, and Alicia and I walked there. Anyone game?"

"Yeah, sure. Sounds good. We'll pick a day soon," we all agreed.

"OK, but you can't tell anyone else, all right? The owner will get really mad at us for leaving the camp."

So we had a secret to keep. From my personal experience, secrets come back to bite you in the ass.

Up at the crafts cabin, I brightened my Linda mood by doing a painting for Mom while Jane tried her hand at the potter's wheel. I misjudged the separation of space needed for our opposing talents, and Jane had the watery clay slip flying everywhere, including on my painting.

"Hey," I yelled, giggling as she kept throwing the dirty water at me.

Jane hooted, "Now, that's a realistic landscape with mud in it."

I couldn't stop laughing at how Jane's clothes and face where soaked when Andrew Finnegan came in seeing us sling clay at each other.

He walked by my table and stopped to look at my watercolor.

"That's a good painting. Too bad there's clay all over it," he said, offering a big smile.

I was embarrassed about acting so ridiculous in front of this really cute guy. All I could get out was, "Thanks," as I tried to casually wipe the mud off my face.

He sat down at another table with some paper and charcoal and started sketching. Jane and I cleaned up our mess on the floor and put everything away. I looked back at him to wave goodbye, but he was focused on his drawing. I wondered if he had a girlfriend.

I went to the bathhouse to get cleaned up. Linda was sitting on a shower bench crying while carving into her arm with a craft knife.

I ran to her with paper towels, shocked at the lines in her skin.

"Linda, why are you doing this?"

"I don't like myself very much," she said quietly. "You know why."

"Jesus, Linda, just 'cause I trashed you over a snide comment doesn't mean you should go to this extreme," I protested. "Are you getting any help for cutting yourself?"

"I was in therapy with someone at home. My parents fight all the time. It's an escape for me. I feel better when I do it. Mom thought I'd stop if I was in a good place."

"Now I get the long sleeves," I said looking at her scars.

"Yeah, well keep it to yourself, please," she answered.

"I'm not leaving you here like this. We all have our problems, but you've got to find a different way to feel better. Clean yourself up. I'll go with you to the cabin, and I won't say anything now. I'll keep your secret only if you get some help. Set up a FaceTime with your shrink or call her while you're here."

She didn't reply.

"I mean it, Linda. No one should have to suffer like that. Promise you'll call."

"I'll think about it."

After dinner, the campers gathered around the fire pit toasting marshmallows and making smores. On our way back to

114

Seneca, I noticed Linda was walking by herself, so I took her arm to catch up with the rest of the girls.

When we came in the door, we heard, "Clean this mess up now!" from both counselors. Our cabin was a disaster from an earlier sock and underwear war, but I caught Brianna smiling and shaking her head.

Why didn't this fun week ease my confusion toward the person who tossed me aside? I took out my notepad and started a list of questions to Keira Tierney: 1. Why didn't you care? Then I wrote a letter to my mom, because she did care.

Our cell phones had to stay in the cabin, so on Sunday of the second week, I found a message Dad left me while we were riding. "Phoebe, I'd like you to come back for an appointment with Dr. Landt on one of your Saturday's coming up. Please call me back."

He picked up right away. "Hi, PS," he said. "I'm so glad to hear from you."

"How is Mom? Can I speak to her yet?"

"You should try to call her tomorrow. Remember that her illness is not permanent. She'll get better, but just give her time with the right people. I need to know your appointment date for Dr. Landt."

I said, "I'll make it for August 5, the week before the horse show. Have you talked to Drew? Maybe he could pick me up then if you're busy," knowing I was sounding sarcastic.

He ignored my comment. "Mrs. Sinks called me yesterday about your thank you letter. That was very nice, Phoebe. She appreciated it, especially the drawing of Jasmine on the back. Drew had a call back from one of the interviews. This one is in

New York, so keep your fingers crossed. How is camp going for you?"

"It's great when I'm busy, especially the riding. At night I just get in a bad mood. I'm here and not helping, and Mom's locked up."

"Phoebe, I understand your concern, but try not to brood about it. You offer your mom support when you speak with her. She doesn't want you worrying. It's better if she knows you're having a good summer, not a fretful one."

"I'll call the hospital after we hang up. I've got some letters to mail her about the riding program and the instructor, Mrs. Tully. She's a good teacher."

Dad said, "I'm so glad to hear that. I included carrots for the horses in the care package you requested."

"Thanks."

"About Mrs. Lorrenze…"

I wished he could see my eyes roll. "Dad, how can you still want to be with Mom's BEST FRIEND after her blabbing everything to Jackie? That was horrible. You just don't understand how cruel she is…and this whole thing with Keira Tierney." I was getting really worked up.

"Phoebe, stop. You're going to have to accept it. There are some problems I'll tell you about when I see you later. You're my priority, and I love you, PS. That won't change."

I hung up on him. I'd never done that, but I just couldn't talk to him any more about who he chose to be with. I was trying to hide that I was crying when we hung up, but Jane came over and sat on the bed.

She poked me, "You have the strangest moods. Is something the matter?"

"It's my mom. She's in the hospital, and I'm worried about her. That's why my dad sent me to camp this summer. He doesn't want me back home when he's hooking up with my mom's best friend."

Her jaw dropped as she handed me a tissue, and we sat together for a minute.

"That sucks for your mom. You should make something and send it to her. Would she like that?" Jane asked.

I gave her a sly look, "I'll throw a pot for her."

"Oh, really? You want some help?" That made me laugh.

On Monday morning of the second week, I called the hospital and had to leave a message for Dr. Gordon. I put my phone back in my duffle and went to the barn.

Susan Banks from Iroquois cabin joined our equestrian group, and she was clearly an experienced rider. She had short blond hair, was thin and very athletic. We traded horse show stories and learned that Susan had entered and won a lot of ribbons around the Fairfield County, Connecticut area where

Robin was from. Pam and Jane were from Tarrytown and Chappaqua, both towns nearly bordering Maple Ridge, and I was surprised to find out that Jane's best friend took a few of the same art classes as I did. We talked about places we'd gone to in New York City, and I mentioned a few jazz clubs I was familiar with.

Our riding group spent a good amount of our days at the barn cleaning up. We helped with mucking out the stalls, watering the horses, and turn-out. Whenever Frank saw us with our rakes and wheelbarrow, he liked to say, "Here come the Barn Rats," and we'd laugh and throw hay at him.

Every day we learned something new. Before we mounted up, we were quizzed on the anatomy of a horse, the consequences of riding too long or too hard, and the importance of proper feed. Mrs. Tully and Frank checked the pastures weekly to get rid of any poisonous weeds that a horse could eat. A lot of plants can cause severe illness or death if ingested. Bracken fern, hemlock, oleander, and red maple leaves are only a few of the problem species.

Tuesday afternoon, the five of us sat outside the barn at a picnic table eating lunch with Mrs. Tully.

"How did you become a trainer?" asked Jane.

"I always liked working with kids and was a teaching assistant at a nearby school which left the summers free. During the school year, I volunteered at the SPCA in my town and was told of a stable with a therapeutic riding program. Then the Riding Director position opened up a couple of years ago here and it's worked out for me."

I said, "Oh, there's a therapy class at the stable where I go. They started working with wounded veterans recently. It's amazing what a difference riding can make for someone."

We started talking about some of the horse shows we had gone to and were surprised that Mrs. Tully had been a Junior Equestrian runner-up. She said, "The National Horse Show is now in Kentucky, but when I rode my horse, Will-Do, it was held at Madison Square Garden in New York City. I was competing for Medal class in the Junior Equestrian under eighteen division."

She told us that when she was competing to be a finalist she had to qualify by winning three Maclay classes or three Medal classes in sanctioned horse shows. "Back then, in my division, I had to compete over a course of eight jumps followed by the top ten to fifteen riders being called back. The final group rode on the flat, just walk, trot and canter – no jumps, and then again we were judged on the rider's form. For the Equitation Medal class, we did a course of jumps, and the top four riders were called back, traded horses as the judge directed, and jumped the course again."

"Holy cow, so you were one of the top four riders that year," Pam said.

"Are the fences we're doing now similar to the ones in the Equitation Medal class?" I asked.

Mrs. Tully answered, "I have mostly verticals set up right now, but I can put up more variation if you girls would like to practice. I think all of you are advanced enough to start going to more sanctioned shows back home. The Medal class is the most prestigious if you're serious."

The afternoon went quickly as we watched some of the group lessons and helped get the feed ready. There is just something about hearing the sound of a bunch of horses in a quiet barn crunching on their oats that's very satisfying.

When we came back to change, I heard my phone beeping. I waved to the girls as they left for a swim. I kept hoping to see Keira's number, and there it was on the screen causing a sudden stabbing pain in my eye. I took a deep breath, exhaled slowly, pressed Accept, and said hello. There was a silent second before hearing, "I'm returning a call from Phoebe. This is Keira Leighton."

"I found a letter," trying not to yell as my heart was pounding, "and a birth certificate I didn't know about. I have some questions."

Brusquely, she said, "Can you hold on please? I have to go to another room."

121

I waited.

"Thanks," she sighed. "I've been thinking about you lately, and wondered if you would call. You sound very grown up."

I didn't care to hear useless compliments. "I want to know if you stayed in contact with my father or mother. If they know where you are."

"No contact from them. But I sent my address in a letter about a year ago."

"So you never really tried to see me."

She sighed again. "I felt it would be inappropriate to confront you without any warning. If I'm guessing correctly, I didn't even exist for you until recently, so your parents probably didn't tell you the truth."

I said, "That's right. I found out by accident that you're my birth mother. Did you know Patrice, my mom?"

"No, I'm afraid not," she said.

"Well, she knew you, and she just had a breakdown because of you."

"I'm sorry to hear that, but how do you think I'm responsible?" Keira asked.

"She's afraid you want me back, but I'll bet that's not true, right?"

"You've had a family for your whole life, Phoebe. Why would you want to change that?"

"That's not the point I'm making. I wondered why you didn't want me fifteen years ago."

"Oh," she said. "There were some problems, and it was complicated. Your father's a good man, but we couldn't get along."

"You mean he didn't like your gambling. Are you still doing that?"

"Not for several years, Phoebe. My family has been wonderfully supportive in getting me help for that."

"When you say family, you mean children?"

"Yes, that's right. Brittney, who answered the phone, and Kevin."

My head really hurt when she said her kids' names. A girl and a boy of her own, and I was the burden she couldn't manage.

"I have to go," and hung up abruptly. I was shaking, partly from anger, but mainly from the pain of rejection. Not a phone call I'd likely forget.

Later, I could barely eat dinner. I left to go back to the cabin to call Sharon. I was so happy she picked up.

I blurted, "I just talked to my birth mother, Keira Leighton. I found out Mom isn't actually my mom."

Sharon was speechless. She could barely get "Oh, my God" out. I tearfully spilled out everything.

"Yup. Nobody ever told me but that isn't the worst of it, because the first hint of the truth was through Jackie Lorrenze. She knew about it. Before I did."

Sharon said, "That was the comment I remember her making at the pool. Well, she deserved your punch to her jaw after all."

"I found a letter from Keira to Mom and my birth certificate. That's how I contacted her. I haven't told anyone else. It just…hurts too much."

"Are you going to talk to your mom?" Sharon asked.

"I can't yet. She'd freak again. Gotta go. Everyone's coming back in," I said.

After our class Wednesday morning, Robin and I told Mrs. Tully we were doing another activity in the afternoon, but we actually went on a hike by ourselves to the country store. We told Pam, Chantel and Jane, but they decided to go another time. We started directly after lunch taking the path from the barn. It was about 80°F and humid in the sunny areas but much better in the shade. The path led through several open fields crossing some tractor tracks, deer paths and streams on the way. We hopped on the rocks to cross a stream and took turns splashing each other. About forty-five minutes later we were downwind from a decrepit two-story house in the middle of a mowed field with junk strewn all over. I would have disregarded it had it not been for the terrible smell that came wafting toward us in a breeze. As we walked closer, noise from dogs was incessant. Not just two, but probably over fifty animals were barking from inside that house.

I looked at Robin in horror and exclaimed, "I can't believe a family can take care of that many dogs."

Robin replied, "When I came by here last summer, I didn't hear so many there. This is awful. The owner must be a hoarder. I wonder why no one's complained." As we looked around, the house had no neighbors and was set back from the road.

We continued on our way for another twenty minutes, climbed a short hill, and saw Up The Creek Country Store just ahead. It was a medium-sized white building with four rocking chairs occupying a long covered porch in front of the front door and looked to be a private home previously. As we entered, we noticed a few local customers chatting with the counter helper. We each bought a water and looked around.

We took a cart and browsed through a few rooms finding lots of different merchandise. Sun tan lotion, bug spray, band-aids, a shower cap that I needed, and a new loofa were added to the basket.

"Oh, look at these quilts." I heard Robin say from the second room. "There are a lot of handmade pillows in here, too." I walked in to spot another table where several artists had a display of earrings.

"These are perfect for a night at the opera," I giggled, holding a pair of huge chandeliers next to my ears.

"Check out those beaded ones. They're really pretty," Robin said, selecting one. "Here, you should get a pair, too."

While I made my choice, I heard Robin say, "Jackpot. Found the baked goods, Phoebe."

We rolled up to the front register with two-dozen cookies, a full cake, plus a few bags of candy, chips, and four magazines along with all the earrings and other sundries, and waited while the clerk tallied the totals for us. As we were leaving, the woman asked, "Are you girls from the camp down the road?"

I had no idea what to say, so we just thanked her and pretended we didn't hear the question as we left. Once outside, I loaded up the backpack with most of our stash and we decided to trade off carrying the large bag with the cake. We trekked the same three-mile route to our cabin, finishing at least two cookies each on the way, and just made it in time to take a shower before the dinner bell, but I couldn't get the noise of the animals in that house out of my mind.

After dinner, as we entered our cabin, I stopped Robin. "I can't help thinking about all those animals in that horrible, smelly house."

"It was awful to see, but what can we do?" she replied. "If we tell someone, we'd be in a lot of trouble for leaving the camp."

I gave her part of my Hershey bar. "I don't know, but I can't ignore it."

I pulled my cell from my duffle and pressed Sharon's number. She had left a message earlier about her trip.

She picked up and I yelled, "It's just not the same riding without you here!"

"Yeah, I miss you, too. How're you doing?" she asked.

"I hate myself for being angry at Mom. The big secret was her idea and it's all been a big effing lie."

"She must have been scared Keira would take you back."

"Why does telling the truth seem so hard to people?"

"It happens all the time. We didn't know my dad was going to leave until he walked out the door. So, call me if you get upset again, OK?"

"Yeah, will do. Thanks."

Thursday, I was determined to switch my focus from Keira to the ASPCA and local animal shelters for information on reporting that dog house. I was able to find two sites and called Robin over.

"I'm calling the number they have here, to learn what the process is for helping the dogs," I said.

Robin said, "That makes sense. Get a pencil so you can write down the time and person you speak to."

The ASPCA suggested looking for the local shelter in the area. I called them next. I asked, "How do I report a terrible animal hoarding situation?"

The volunteer replied, "You need the location and the name of the owner to make the report. In some cases the police have to be involved if the situation poses a health risk."

I took her name and said I'd get back to her with more information. Somehow, I was going to help those animals.

Friday morning came, and we were up and ready for our lesson. The five "Barn Rats" finished a great scrambled eggs and sausage breakfast and walked to the barn at the top of the hill. We said hi to Frank and Eddie, the grubby, hay delivery guy. I'd seen him several times helping Frank around the barn.

We were very surprised to see some new jumps in the meadow. Mrs. Tully and Frank had set up several fences at two feet nine inches including an ascending oxer, a coup, a parallel oxer, two vertical fences with flowers at the base, one plain vertical, two crossrails, plus two walls measuring a height of three feet. After explaining the course of eight that we were to practice today, we were shown how to pace off the striding for the jumps. Because the average horse has a twelve foot stride, we measured the fences to be set apart by twelve foot increments.

We worked for thirty minutes on the flat and let the horses get accustomed to the new fences. We jumped three with Mrs. Tully critiquing each rider, but when we continued with the full course, I kept thinking of my mess-up with Doris at Maple Hill. Sure enough, I had to circle twice before Kahlua would clear the walls. The last part of the lesson was a cool down with exercises on horseback. Was Keira Leighton the problem? Was she the reason I couldn't get past thinking I wasn't good enough?

Kahlua had become my favorite horse to ride, a handsome 15.3 dark buckskin quarter horse with a dorsal stripe down his back. Robin chose the slightly taller buckskin, Maroo, who was almost identical to Kahlua. Jane liked to ride Felix, a dapple gray. Pam chose Rowdy, a chestnut cool guy, and Susan was smitten with Secret Victory, a 16.0 spicy bay. Susan rode quietly with steady hands helping to calm his energy.

Robin and I dismounted and removed tack quickly, then led Maroo and Kahlua to the turn out. As we watched the horses grazing, I looked over to Robin.

"I have to say something about that house with all the animals. I can't imagine the mess inside. I'm gonna give Mrs. Tully the information I have now and see if she can help me get the location and name of the owner. She worked with the local SPCA, and maybe she knows someone to call there. I won't mention you were there at all. I just have to speak up."

Robin thought for a minute. "We could be in trouble for leaving."

"That's why I won't say you were with me. I got lost on a hike."

"No. We'll go together. I feel bad about the animals, too."

We found Mrs. Tully in one of the stalls.

"Uh, Mrs. Tully? We have to tell you something, and it will probably get us in some trouble," I said.

She put the pitchfork aside and tilted her head a notch. "What's the problem?"

"Well, we were on a hike, and we came across a horrible situation involving a lot of hoarded animals in a little house. It was pretty awful and when I called the Humane Society, I found out we need the specific address. You worked for the local SPCA, right? Do they step in to remove them if there is a complaint?"

She said, "Did you ask your counselor about it already?"

"Well," I mumbled. "We went on a hike just the two of us. And got lost."

Mrs. Tully looked sharply at us. "You went off by yourselves. In the woods. Without telling anyone?"

I looked at Robin. She reasoned, "We couldn't let the situation just go and not tell what we saw. Can you please check on the dogs? This is the shelter we called. They need their name and the address. You could get the town records pretty easily."

"I'll have to look at the place myself first before notifying the shelter. Since I don't know the location, I guess you two are going to go with me," she said pointedly.

We looked hopeful for two seconds, until she added, "This does not in any way mean that your action of leaving the camp was wise."

She called the camp office and said she was going to take the two of us to look at one of the trails.

We climbed in the truck, but we weren't sure how far along the main road it was. "I think we walked for about forty minutes through the fields and woods before we got there. So that's about two miles." We kept the windows down and drove slowly to see if we could hear the dogs.

"We must be getting close to the house by now," I said. I saw a stream by the road and thought that could have been the one we crossed.

"So, how did you like the Up The Creek Country Store on your hike, girls?" Mrs. Tully asked looking over at the two of us.

Oh boy, we'd been made.

Just then, I heard the barking. There was a narrow driveway that led through a bunch of trees. We drove in for about twenty feet and continued slowly. The house was there. Mrs. Tully got out and looked at the mess around the yard while the sickening odor came in through the car windows. She returned to the driver's seat and said, "All right, I've seen enough. It's a nightmare."

She noted the color of the mailbox and location of the driveway. She took out her phone and snapped videos of the house, showing dogs in the windows. We drove back in silence and pulled in at the dining hall. "You girls go back to your cabin."

We took our time walking to Seneca. We had missed lunch while looking for the house, but we were more worried about the consequences of leaving camp.

"Thanks for deciding to come with me," I said to Robin.

"I wonder what Mrs. T. will do to us."

Our bunkmates filtered in following their Friday afternoon activities. We had stashed our booty from the store trip on Wednesday on one of the upper shelves, and when all the girls returned, we broke out some of the good candy and the rest of the cake. I noticed that Linda stayed on her bed reading.

"Hey," I said handing her a paper plate. "We have cake over there. Why don't you get a piece?"

I'd noticed that she had stopped the remarks and hopefully no more cutting herself.

She looked at me not sure whether to say something. After a minute, she said, "Thanks, I think I will."

A bit awkward, but we had to share the cabin for five more weeks, so it was a start.

At dinner, our group followed the scent of the barbequed chicken dinner to the dining hall. There was a clever banjo player making up songs from phrases the girls gave him, and he was pretty good.

We were ready for lights out, but I kept thinking about the dog hell house in the field, wondering what went through people's minds to be able to live in such filthy conditions with no regard for the well being of their animals. I hoped that the dogs might eventually be able to find good homes.

Sunday went by quickly. Chantel and I volunteered to look for new trails with Frank and Eddie before the games and swimming races started in the afternoon. We hadn't heard from Mrs. Tully, but she generally took the weekends off.

During Monday's breakfast of pancakes and bacon, Mrs. Finnegan asked the Seneca and Iroquois cabins to stay behind.

A huge cheer broke out when she announced that the two cabins with girls ages thirteen to sixteen could go to Six Flags this week with permission from their parents. We were all jumping up and down because Robin and Alicia went last year and said it was dy-no-mite.

When I returned to Seneca, I heard my phone buzz. I was so surprised it was Mom saying she was home. She sounded pretty good at first with questions about the camp and riding. As I answered one question she immediately had another. I finally asked her if everything was all right because she seemed so excitable and distracted.

"Phoebe, I've never felt better. I'm fine, and as soon as I see you, I have it all planned that we'll go on a vacation together. I am getting tickets for us to go to Savannah, Georgia to see my cousin. I've already talked to her, and we should go next week."

"Uh, that...is a surprise, Mom, but I'm at camp until August 18. We should go after that, because it's paid for already."

"Phoebe, did you not hear me? We are going to Savannah and that is final. I have some calls to make. I will talk to you later."

She hung up.

I was mystified by how she spoke to me. Rarely did Mom lose her patience or cool. This was un-cool.

I called my dad to apologize for hanging up the week before.

"You know, Phoebe, no one feels more beat up than I do about what happened to Mom. Do I feel responsible? I'm sure, in some ways I did not help. I can't turn back the clock, either. So we're all trying our best to get her back to 100 percent, but all this pressure is piling up on you. That's what hurts the most, PS. Please, let this summer be at least halfway good for you, OK? So, what's going on there?"

"Dad, everything about the camp is so much more than I expected. We go to Six Flags on Thursday."

"That's great, Phoebe, you'll have more fun with your friends than with me. I'm sorry it didn't work out last July when we were supposed to go. Are you homesick yet?"

Thank goodness Mrs. Tully didn't tell him we took an unscheduled walk.

"The only problem is this killer poison ivy on my legs." I didn't mention it was probably from our six-mile hike last week. I added, "The nurse is taking care of it with lots of calamine lotion."

I told him about Kahlua, the horse I was riding.

He replied, "You always do well when you like it. Do you need any more clothes?"

I said, "No, thanks. The last package you sent had everything. Especially the Cheez-Whiz and chocolates."

He sounded a little down. I asked, "Is Mom doing OK at home now? I called earlier, but she didn't pick up."

There was a pause. "What do you mean at home?" he asked.

"Mom called and said she was out of the hospital, and she's at home."

"Oh, my God. Uh, Phoebes, I have to go. Love you, PS." He hung up.

"But, Dad, I didn't finish," I said to a dead phone.

Robin heard the conversation and looked over, "What's going on?"

"I think Dad didn't know that Mom is out of the hospital. He's the contact, so I don't know how that happened."

Later, the girls and I went to the barn and spent the whole day there except for lunch. Mrs. Tully wasn't there, so Monday lessons were canceled. Frank was there with Eddie doing some carpentry work. We asked if it was OK to ride, and he gave us the go ahead. After an hour of walking around the ring, I saw Linda coming up to watch us. I motioned her to come over.

"Do you want to try it?" Pam asked.

"I was only on a birthday party pony one time. Is it safe?" Linda asked.

I said, "We'll walk with you. See if you like it."

She climbed over the fence and came up to Maroo to give him a pat on the neck.

Robin dismounted and helped Linda hike into the saddle.

"Here, you hold the reins like this," as she showed Linda and shortened the stirrups for her.

"Now, sit up and try to keep your heels down."

Jane and Felix stayed on her left side as they walked with Linda around the ring.

"Now pick up the reins like this, and we'll go for a trot." Jane said.

At first, Linda was flopping all over the place, but she got the hang of posting by the time she made it around one time. They walked again while Jane said, "Now we'll canter together. It's a much smoother gait. Turn Maroo's nose toward the rail and bump him with your inside leg."

Jane stayed next to Linda circling the ring in a nice slow canter. I'd never seen Linda's face show such delight in anything before. When they came back to the center, Linda exclaimed, "Oh, my gosh, he's like a rocking horse! That was so much fun! I was like flying!"

Jane took her for another turn before we had to finish. Linda had found something to do. Would that make the difference in cutting herself, I wondered? She stayed to help us turn them out in the paddock and muck out the stalls.

"Do you think I could sign up for lessons?" she asked.

I said, "Come up tomorrow to see Mrs. Tully. You have to get permission for the program from your parents, and she can tell you if maybe there's a spot open in Chantel's group."

It was the first time I'd seen Linda excited about anything. One horseback ride may have changed her world.

When I got back to Seneca, I saw there were three messages on my phone.

The first voicemail was from Mom. "Phoebe, everything is arranged, and I'm coming to pick you up at camp. You are to get all your things together ready to come back with me."

The second was from my Dad. "Phoebe, call me as soon as you get this."

The third was also from Dad with the same message. I pressed Call and waited.

"Phoebe, this is important. Your mother is not supposed to be away from the hospital. Have you heard from her today?"

"Well, yes. She left a message about an hour ago that I just got. I'm confused, Dad. Camp isn't over for a month, and she's taking me away from here. She's on her way now to bring me home. How did she get out of the hospital?"

"Please listen. I'm driving there now. She is going to have to return for treatment. You should not leave camp with her. I spoke to Mrs. Finnegan and explained the situation. Please don't leave your cabin right now. When did she say she was coming?"

"The message was left an hour ago, so she must be half way here by now."

"Text me and try to stall her when she gets there. If she insists that you leave, call me, and I'll talk to her myself. I'll try to call you on the way."

Robin came back with some fruit for me, but my tummy was so upset I could barely get an apple down. Where was Mom? I felt sick. Mom wasn't in her right mind, and I couldn't imagine what her reaction would be if I refused to leave. I was pacing the floor when I called Sharon. She could tell I was upset. "What's wrong?" she said.

I told her, "Mom's on her way here to drive me home, and Dad told me not to leave with her. I just don't see how I can refuse. I'll have to go if she throws a fit or something and figure out what to do on the way back."

Sharon considered, "Maybe you can talk her out of it and have her stay there overnight. Or, like he said, keep talking to her until your dad comes."

"Yeah. It's mostly his fault in the first place."

Sharon came back with, "Phoebe, I can tell you're angry. Try to calm down."

"I wish you were here to help, Shar. It's late, and I don't know where my mom is. I'll call you back tomorrow."

Robin offered as I put my phone away, "She probably changed her mind, Phoebe, or she had to stop somewhere. I'm sure she'll call you about what happened. There must be a very good reason why she isn't here yet."

"I can't talk about it right now, OK?" snapping back at her.

I saw Robin look at Jane with palms up and shrug.

We ended up getting showered and ready for bed. I tried Dad and left him a voicemail. It was time for lights out, so Mom was definitely not coming.

I was wiped out. I cried quietly until I fell asleep.

Tuesday morning it poured. After breakfast a lot of the girls went to the dining hall to watch a movie, but for me it was too noisy and nerve wracking to be with other kids. I was surprised that Jane was willing to stay with me in the cabin and play cards. I was not in a good mood. We finished the rest of the care package my Dad sent and watched the rain pelt the windows.

My phone rang. It was Drew. I hadn't thought to call him during this current mess but was optimistic he'd spoken with Dad.

"Hi, Phoebes, how're you doing?"

"Worried. Do you have any news?"

"Yes, actually, I do," Drew said. "Patrice learned the code for a side door when she saw a nurse leave. Then she walked to one of the nearby stores and called a cab to take her home. They didn't discover her missing until later."

"Mom never got here. Where is she?"

"I'm sorry, Phoebe, but Patrice was stopped for speeding in Massachusetts. There was a problem when they pulled her over. She became very agitated, and she was taken into custody for disorderly conduct."

Instant headache. Had to sit on the bed. Holy shit.

"She was arrested? Where is she now?"

"No arrest. They released her to be taken by ambulance back to White Plains. Anyway, I drove Dad to get Patrice's car. He's driving it back to Maple Ridge now."

Silence.

"Phoebe? You still there?"

"Uh. Yeah. When's she going to get better?"

He couldn't answer that. Instead he offered, "Hey, I'm not too far from the camp. Would you like me to stop by?"

I struggled getting "OK" out, and pulled three tissues from the box.

"It'll be about thirty minutes."

The rain stopped on my way to the dining hall to meet Drew. I was crying badly when he walked over to give me a hug.

The movie was over, the hall cleared out, so we sat down and talked.

"She's going to be better. You just have to give her time," he said.

I motioned, "Let's go to the barn," as I wiped my face. "It's easier to think there."

We toured the camp on the way, and I showed him my cabin. When we were near the barn, I saw Mrs. Tully's truck.

I said, "Come on, I'll introduce you."

Mrs. Tully came out and said hi to Drew on our way to Kahlua's stall.

I asked her if we could take Rowdy and Kahlua into the meadow for a little while.

We spent most of the time walking the horses in the sunshine. Here was Drew again when I needed someone.

"I feel guilty having such a great summer when Mom is in such a bad way."

Drew said, "That's because you're a good person. If you didn't feel upset, I wouldn't be here for you."

"Do you have a job yet?" I asked.

"Still haven't heard. But I have two more interviews next week."

I asked, "Will you go to see your friend on the way back? You never said who it is."

"It's a she. We started dating last year. And, yes, I'll stop by her place. Let's change the subject. I think you should take a few of those nice jumps for me."

Drew on Rowdy stayed in the middle of the ring while Kahlua and I warmed up. We did a few circles around the fences and went over the verticals with flowers and foliage, two oxers, and changed direction to the taller vertical, but I stopped before going to the wall.

Drew said, "Equitation is when the rider is judged on her form, not the horse, correct?"

I went to the center. "Yes, you remembered."

"Well, you look mah-ve-lous. Nice quiet seat and hands, heels down, looking for the next one to sail over. When's the horse show?"

"August 12. Maybe you can come that day."

"Can't promise." He cocked his head, "But maybe. So how come you didn't take on the walls?"

I thought for a sec. "They're solid and look dangerous even though I know these are wood. They're around the same height, but more unyielding I think. Kahlua will do all these by himself.

It's so funny to watch when he's turned out. He canters around and does the whole course."

We started putting the horses away and said goodbye to Mrs. Tully.

After taking the horses to their stalls, I said to Drew, "Mom was coming here to pick me up to go to her cousin's in Savannah. Why would she suddenly want to go there?"

Drew snapped a look toward me and stopped. "What trip to Savannah?"

"That's why Mom was coming here. She had tickets and made arrangements already."

"You'll have to speak to Dad about that. I didn't hear anything."

I walked Drew back to his car, feeling alone and angry, and I let my tears go again. Drew hugged me and waited till I stopped. He said, "There's nothing wrong with crying sometimes. You'll feel better after."

I said, "OK, good to know."

Drew advised, "And don't hold back when you talk to Dad. He needs a good tongue-lashing, I think."

"That item's been checked off already."

The rest of Tuesday was not good. When I went back to the cabin, I found Robin talking to Pam and Chantel, and I thought it was about me.

144

"What's going on? I just heard my name."

"Phoebe, I was just wondering if you are OK. You've been crying at night about your mom. We're just worried about you."

"Well, don't. And please stop talking behind my back about me or my family. I don't like that. You wouldn't either. Just leave me alone, will you?"

I grabbed my towel because I had nowhere to go except the showers. I tried to use the breathing exercise Dr. Landt told me. I guess I hadn't practiced enough.

Everyone left for dinner. I stayed put.

Wednesday was one week since we saw the hoarder cabin. Following breakfast, I went to the barn for the lesson and found Robin and the others were already waiting for Mrs. Tully.

Robin said, "Yo', Bitch. I see you got your mad face on still."

"I'll get over it if you leave me alone."

Robin came back with, "Cut out the crapola or we're not speaking to you for the rest of the week. You've got one hour to shape up, Missy."

Mrs. Tully called us to the barn. She gave me that steely look and said, "Get rid of the attitude." That's when I really knew I was behaving badly.

The five of us did the course a number of times, and I was at the front line of Mrs. Tully's firing range because of the wall jumps again.

"Phoebe, your mood is stinking up the barn. Do NOT take it out on your horse," she said loudly, as I pulled too sharply on the reins. She continued quizzing us on horse anatomy and when we got something wrong, there were no excuses. She would ask us again until we got it right. We removed tack and finished walking the sweat off us and the horses.

"Mrs. Tully, we won't be here tomorrow for our lesson," Pam said. "We're all going to Six Flags."

"Well, you girls have a great time. And Phoebe, stay a minute, please."

Oh, crap. I glared when everybody looked at me, then turned away quickly.

Mrs. Tully warned, "With all your experience, being on a horse should make you feel energized and uplifted. I'm not seeing that at all. I understand there are some problems you're having, but don't punish the horse, or for that matter, the people who care about you."

"Yes, Mrs. Tully," I answered quietly.

"Also, I'm sure you're anxious to hear about the dogs. I don't have any news yet. When I'm given an update on the situation, I'll let you know."

"Thanks, Mrs. Tully."

I followed the girls to the pool knowing I had to handle these awful disappointments better. I didn't want to feel angry about Dad or Mom, or take it out on the girls.

CHAPTER 12   THE PARK

Thursday morning the two cabins assembled at the dining hall for instructions. At Six Flags, we could choose to be divided into teams of two, three, or four to check in with our counselor by phone. If anyone had a problem, the counselor should be notified right away. Sixteen girls and six counselors plus Andrew and his friend, Jeff, all boarded the school bus.

Everyone on the bus was yelling, "JOKER, JOKER," for the new roller coaster. More like a NASA training program from what I heard. I wasn't too sure really, about ninety degree drops and free flying while your seat flips around multiple times. If you go, it better be on an empty stomach.

There was a discount for the park tickets purchased in advance that allowed us to enter quickly. Most of the campers chose to ride Joker first. There was a long line there and would probably increase later on. Robin and I were chicken, but Pam and Jane were game for it.

I knew that no one really wanted to be with me, but Robin spoke up. "Phoebe and I are going to start at Thunderbolt. We'll catch up with you later." The wooden coaster had no loopy-loops, but the ride is so much rougher because the cars bounce and vibrate along the track. It sure did shake a lot of my tension loose.

Next we tried Catwoman's Whip, mostly for the smaller kids. It was slower, but the curves made it feel really fast. I was starting to have fun, but I knew I was being a pain in the ass. I said, "You know, you're the only one who's put up with my crap recently."

"Yeah, I can see it slowly melting away," making drippy motions with her fingers. "Maybe you'll turn into a human again by the end of the night," as she grimaced.

I made a goofy face.

When we walked past Bizarro, the one that goes 77 mph, I taunted Robin saying, "I'll wait for you if you want to go," never thinking she'd do it. I was so shocked when she said, "OK!" and trotted over to join the line.

I was looking around for a place to get a soda when Andrew and his friend came up from behind and surprised me. "You're Phoebe, aren't you? Have you gone on any of the rides yet?"

"Yes. We just got off Catwoman's Whip, and Robin is over there," I pointed, "at Bizarro. I'm waiting for her."

149

"I'm Andrew, and that's Jeff. We're going over to Thunderbolt if you want to come," he said.

"I've seen you at camp a couple of times. Robin should be done soon, she's almost at the front now, if you want to wait for us." We stood for a moment looking at each other. "Um, how did you know who I am?" I asked.

"I've been at the stable a couple of times and saw you riding. Frank kept telling me your name was 'Barn Rat', but he finally gave it up."

I admitted, "I knew your name, too. You and Jeff kind of stand out at a girl's camp," I said looking up at him with my best smile.

Andrew was about five feet ten, had short, dark hair, brown eyes, and a fabulous smile. I've noticed that sometimes when talking to people, their eyes flick away at any little distraction. Andrew's focus was only on my face as we spoke.

I asked, "Do you ride, because I haven't seen you while we're helping at the barn?"

"I go early in the morning usually before breakfast. It's nice and cool then, fewer bugs. Mrs. Tully's OK with it."

We both turned toward Bizarro to clearly hear Robin, screaming in fright or hysteria from the first 220 foot drop. "Well, I hope she's having a good time up there," I said, laughing.

150

We talked about riding and other sports until Robin walked back to us. Her usual perfectly straight blond hair looked like a jet had exhaled on it. "The guys are going to walk over to Thunderbolt with us," I said as I gave her a mirror.

"Robin, do you know Jeff?" I asked her.

"Hi," she said. "I've seen you at camp."

Robin took in Jeff's wavy, sandy hair, and blue eyes with dark eyebrows. He was about five feet nine, very fit with muscular legs, and had a vague resemblance to a famous teen singer.

We talked as we walked. "Where do you go to school, Andrew?"

He said, "I live with my dad in Greenwich, Connecticut, where Jeff and I go to a private school. I'll be a senior. How about you?"

"I'll be a sophomore. I like art, but it's hard to fit into my schedule. So I take art club after school. Here we are. The line looks about thirty minutes. Not bad." We watched the people coming off the ride, wearing the biggest smiles or throwing up in the nearest trashcan.

Robin and I spent the rest of the afternoon with the boys, getting snacks, buying souvenirs, and finally going to the Wicked Cyclone. That was a rock and roll, curvy fast one. We took pictures together with the characters wandering around.

"Have you thought about colleges yet?" I asked.

151

"I've focused on three I prefer. I'll be touring some more in the fall with Mom. Yale is my first choice at the moment, but I'm not sure if I can compete with all the superstars who apply. What about you?"

I replied, "I'd like to do something with art or maybe with social work. My Mom works with a human services office in Maple Ridge, NY, where we live. She loves her job, so I've been thinking about that, too."

"Hey, you aren't far from Greenwich. We should go riding together sometime," he said looking right at me.

I hoped he would say that.

It was after six and we wanted food. We heard that Johnny Rockets had very good burgers and were not too bad price-wise, so that's where we went. We split the check four ways and still had time to check out the less awesome rides. Robin and Jeff were right behind us when I stopped short.

"Wait! We have to go on the carousel. That's been my favorite ride since I was little." We walked over to the Illions Grand Carousel with the beautiful antique carved saddle horses. The three watched me hurry toward the fiery black horse on the outside, so Andrew caught up and took the middle one. I snapped photos of Robin and Jeff looking cute sitting together in the chariot making faces and holding hands.

"That was the best ride all night," I yelled. I was walking backwards taking a last look at the carved animals when I accidently smacked hard into someone. My apology came up short when my five feet ten inch worst nightmare was staring down at me.

"You just can't stop screwing up, Bitch!" Jackie said as she shoved me away. For added effect, she wiped off the glob of her ice cream cone that smeared her shirt and threw it on me.

"Hey!" I yelled as I came at her. "What's wrong with you, Jackie? I never did anything to you! Your mom was my mom's BEST FRIEND. Who does that? Blame the person who's responsible, and stop calling me BITCH!"

She pointed and yelled back making even more people stop and watch the scene, "Phoebe, you're gonna be some inmate's bitch when you and your mom are in jail for spending money that's not yours!"

I was horrified by another public confrontation and furious at Jackie's snickering ally, who I recognized from the pizza day fiasco. I stomped off, grabbing Andrew's arm before he interfered. I could tell he was about to say something to her, and I couldn't pull him away fast enough.

Robin and Jeff trailed after us calling, "Who was that?"

Andrew stood in front of me. "Explain, please?"

"Do you have a couple of hours to spare?" I started to cry.

"Whoa," Andrew said. "Whoever that was, she's not worth one more second of your thoughts."

"One of the reasons I went to camp was to get away from that girl!" I sobbed pointing in her direction.

Andrew handed me a handkerchief. "OK. We're away from her now. Let's wrap up this night."

The confrontation stayed with me. What did Jackie mean by "spending money that wasn't ours?" Maybe Mom was on a buying spree, but Jackie wouldn't know that…unless it filtered down from Dad.

I was completely distracted while we did some souvenir shopping. Andrew and Jeff tried on hats while Robin bought a couple of funny t-shirts. My embarrassment kept lingering like a swampy mist. Jacked-up Jackie could sure put a damper on a good evening.

I pulled Andrew aside, "I really want to talk to you about what happened, but not now. I hope you understand."

We stopped to get a soda to take home, when Andrew handed me a small bag. "Will this make you feel better?" he asked.

I opened it to find a carved little black carousel horse he'd bought in one of the shops.

"Andrew, you're amazing. You make me feel better just being here. You know that, right?"

He leaned in for a kiss. I returned it.

The four of us joined the other kids at the entrance just in time to board the bus. Robin and Jeff took the seats opposite us as Jane and Pam used the raised eyebrows signal for details later.

The day at the park had been so nice compared to dates that Sharon and I had put up with in the past. Andrew clearly enjoyed my company unlike the immature boys at school who seemed only interested in what or how much you would do for them.

When we made it back to camp, the counselors were watching, so Robin and I accepted a quick hug goodnight from our sort-of-dates. Andrew said, "I'm looking forward to riding with you soon, Phoebe."

"OK, sounds like a plan."

Bright and early Friday morning Robin threw a pillow at my head because I wouldn't rise when the morning bell gonged. Everyone chimed in, "Happy Birthday, Phoebe!" On this morning no one ventured to breakfast. Even Brianna and Martina seemed reluctant to join the living.

Eventually, there was shuffling around the cabin. Then Dad called. "Happy birthday, young lady. Did you have a good time yesterday?"

"Hi, Dad. I sent you some photos from the trip. The rides were great and we're all pretty tired." He had received my before-and-after shots of Robin and me in front of the coasters (minus the boys) and sounded happy that I had fun.

He said, "There's one more thing I think you'll like. It's about Mom. I already called the head nurse at the hospital and she is expecting you to call your mother Saturday. She's still having trouble holding on to a conversation but Dr. Gordon's not as concerned about her taking off."

"He doesn't think she'll try to leave again?" I asked.

156

"She's had a turn-around. It seems she's trying to work with the doctors so she can get home soon."

I thanked him and hung up.

Hot and humid were the key weather words. The riding lesson went well even though we had Thursday off. Mrs. Tully worked us on the flat for twenty-five minutes. "Nice job with stirrups, ladies. Now it's time to go without them." We stopped and crossed the stirrups over the saddle and continued working through changing leads and direction. We replaced them for the jumping session and found the practice without them had been very helpful.

The pool was on my schedule for the afternoon, and that was cool. The team practiced a synchronized back layout with ballet leg position. I did have an advantage for this because my body floated easily without scuttling.

Sharon called me for my birthday in the afternoon, and I was really happy to hear from her.

"Oh, Sharon, the other day when Mom was coming to camp to take me to Savannah and she never got here? Drew told me she pulled a Houdini from the hospital. No one knew she called a cab to get home till way later." I told her about Mom's police incident and then about Drew coming to see me.

"Have you called her since then?"

"No. Saturday I will. I never asked you about your mom the other day. Is she still really busy?"

"Oh, yeah," Sharon said. "The big Tudor house closed. How was the park yesterday?"

"We went on most of the rides, and I spent the day with Andrew. I think he wants to go riding with me."

"As long he doesn't replace me full time, I'm happy for you," Sharon replied.

I saved Jackie's run-in till last. "I bumped into Jackie last night, literally. I knocked her ice cream on her shirt. She just about attacked me. Sharon, it's like she's stalking me or something."

"That. Is. Weird. Too crazy she'd be there the same day you went."

"I know. Is there any way you can find out from Asia if she heard something about Jackie's timing being at the park? I just can't believe it was a coincidence."

"I'll go to the pool tomorrow, and maybe I'll see her. If not, I'll call her. Speaking of stress, my Dad's wedding is next week in New York. At the Little Church Around the Corner on Twenty-ninth Street. I'm going in for the day."

"I'll talk to you later. Thanks for the birthday wishes."

During the seven weeks at camp there are a lot of birthdays celebrated with cake and ice cream. Even though I'd been a total bitch to everyone, a huge card signed by my cabin mates all decorated inside with hearts, horses and "SENECA" all over it sat waiting for me at the table. The girls had been really patient with my vile attitude. After my fifteen candles were blown out, Mrs. Finnegan came over and said three packages had arrived that afternoon, which she placed on the table. I saved the one from Mom for later, figuring I'd probably get upset. I opened Dad's to find a cool watch that I really liked. The card said, "Miss you, PS. Love, Dad and Drew." Added at the bottom was, "Check your email. There's a link to Cyndi Lauper's *Time After Time*." He remembered that I loved that song. Cool. Sharon's mom sent a gift, too, from both of them. They'd found a beautiful silver snaffle bit bracelet that everybody loved. We ate chocolate cake and ice cream to Chantel's playing pop tunes on her guitar. Great night.

I was curious about what Mom sent, but I waited till we returned to the cabin. The card was pretty, and said, "Thinking of you everyday and love you always, Mom."

I opened the box and found a beautiful little gold horse charm. She had started a bracelet for me when I turned thirteen. I loved it and almost placed it in my jewelry case till I remembered the little gold necklace that I had brought to camp and slipped the horse onto the chain. Perfect. My roommates liked it a lot.

Saturday morning, I called the hospital and was finally able to get through to Mom to thank her for the gold horse.

159

"Ellen found it for me," she said, "and sent it on to you."

I wanted to avoid the Massachusetts police incident and steered the chatting toward riding on the Rockefeller trails. "We have to go together when you're home," I told her.

"I just remembered my horse's name from camp years ago!" Mom exclaimed. "Porsche, because she was so fast. I'd totally forgotten that till just now."

I said, "That sounds like a good sign, Mom. You were almost my age that summer. Did you stay in touch with any of the girls there? I'd like to see my riding group again."

"Just one girl for awhile. I was from the city, and most of the other girls were from Pennsylvania, I think."

"I'll send you pictures of Kahlua. He's great, and I'll be riding him at the show in August."

"I've been taking my meds, Phoebe. Dr. Gordon said my meds were off. That's what happened earlier this week. I won't let it happen again, I promise. I just had to get out of here."

I could hear her crying.

"I have to say you got pretty creative with your escape plan. Why Savannah, Mom? We haven't seen your cousin for ten years at least."

She said, "It was the only place I could think of to take you. I don't want you near Barbara. Dr. Gordon tells me I'm blaming your father. He's wrong. I hold HER responsible."

"Mom, that's not going to do you any good."

"I'm more focused now. I know what she did."

"You mean because Dad left you."

"She did other things, too. I couldn't get proof. I never understood how my best friend could be so cruel and vindictive. She's been after your father and wants me out of the way. Permanently."

"Please, listen to your doctors. I'll call you next week, Mom."

"Phoebe, no. Listen to me. She tried to get me fired from work."

"Mom, I'm coming to see you in two weeks. You can tell me more then."

Could she really be making all this up? At least some parts of it had to be true. I didn't know what to think of her accusations about Barbara Lorrenze. Mom's story might change in two weeks. I figured Dad was the one who started their affair and it wouldn't have been the first time. He still didn't believe me about Jackie's part in this.

Robin and I went to the barn to see if any horses needed exercising. Frank was around and said to take Oscar and Dodi who we'd ridden once before. After doing mostly flat work in the ring, we practiced on some of the low fences in the meadow. We were having such a good time we lost track of how late it was. Robin had promised to call her Dad at four, so we cleaned up, and she went back to the cabin. Frank had to walk down to the camp office below, so I stayed a few minutes to get Oscar and Dodi off the cross ties and into their stalls. I was leaning the manure shovel back in place when I was startled to see Eddie standing at the entry to the barn, watching me.

"I didn't see you there, Eddie," I said uncomfortably. "Frank is just outside," I lied.

He was in his tattered jeans, unshaven, and uncombed. My skin felt prickly being there by myself.

He stepped toward me and said, "You and I know that Frank isn't here, but I think you can help."

The way his dark eyes stared was creepy. He took three more steps forward.

I pointed at him. "Stay there, Eddie, and I'll call him," I warned. I knew I was going to be trapped if I didn't act fast.

He was about ten feet away, so I grabbed the shovel and aimed it toward his chest intending to ram him if I had to. My heart was slamming as I hit him in the mid-section. I took off, tossing the shovel to the side. He was thrown off balance and landed on his butt, which gave me time to get across to the truck parked in the tractor barn. I knew that Frank kept keys under the seat because I saw him store them there.

Run faster, I said to myself. I could hear creepy Eddie back on his feet stomping after me, screaming, "Stop, Barn Rat!" He was too quick. I jumped in the driver's side and locked the door, shaking uncontrollably. "Where are the effing keys, for God's sake?" yelling at myself out loud. Creepy Eddie started banging on the window just as my hand found the key and slipped it in the ignition.

It was a Ram 2500, a few years old. I slammed the clutch to the floor, roared the engine to life, and threw it in reverse. At least I hoped it was reverse, not having driven it before. Hay blew out of the back bed all over the guy as tires were spinning backwards. I popped the clutch. "Crap!" The seat was set too far back, and I could barely reach the pedals, but the truck thankfully had jerked in reverse far enough to be able to turn the wheel. He yelled again when I knocked him to the side as I straightened out. Still shaking, I again jammed the clutch to the floor and shoved the gearshift into first, jerking a couple of times as the clutch caught. In the side mirror, I saw a bunch of dirt and mud blast into Creepy Eddie's face. I thought I could make it to the road now. In second gear, the truck was bouncing along the driveway, and in third gear, the road wasn't any better. There was still a distance to cover with him on the move. My head pounded the ceiling with every pothole, but I didn't lose control. I just kept thudding through the ruts. Once on the road, I cut right and headed directly back to the camp office. This guy needed to be caught. The camp driveway seemed endless, but I sped to the office door, and jumped out.

Frank was in shock and started saying, "What do you think…"

I cut him off yelling, "Eddie just attacked me up there. Call the police! He's probably on the road by now."

He stood there registering what I said. "Hurry, please, Frank."

Mrs. Finnegan came out in a fury, but Frank pulled out his cell and dialed.

They brought me into the office to get a description of Eddie, and I explained that Frank left and I was just finishing up when I saw Eddie at the entrance. I was able to get away, so I was OK, but Creepy Eddie must have been watching for a while.

I was sitting on the sofa with tea, a blanket and four adults standing around. The police station was just down the road, and they actually found the guy and questioned him.

The seriousness of the situation hit me. I just wanted to go back to the cabin. Almost everyone had heard about it by the time Mrs. Finnegan walked me back to Seneca. While lying in bed, questions filled my mind. What if I couldn't have gotten away? What if Frank's truck hadn't been there? I was shaking all over when Jane came over to my bed and sat down. "You OK, Phoebe?" she asked.

I looked up at her and started bawling, "Nooooo." Jane took my hand while grabbing some tissues.

"Let it go, Phoebe. Don't hold it in," she said soothingly. "Listen, last year on a date this guy was supposed to be driving me home, but he took a detour that I didn't want. I fought him off, but it scared the shit out of me. I had a torn shirt, but he ended up with a black eye. I didn't tell anyone about it, and that was a mistake. It took forever to get a grip. So, talk about it, cry about it, but get it out of your system."

"I wasn't hurt. I'm OK. I just can't get the 'what if' out of my head," I said feeling disgusted.

"You'll relive it for awhile. Just remember that you got away, and the guy was caught. All good."

"Thanks, Jane."

I was able to eat a light meal, and after dinner, Mrs. Finnegan took me to the office again. She said, "I called your father and explained what happened today. Eddie's in jail for probation violation, and because of the attack, he won't get bail. Frank didn't know that Eddie has a criminal history, and he feels simply terrible about what happened to you. He was just trying to help him get work."

I started to say, "It wasn't Frank's fault. It was scary, but I got away…" and realized I was shaking again.

She went on. "Sometimes bad experiences can cause problems later on, and your father wanted to make sure you wished to stay and finish the season here."

I looked down at my hands. "I'm fine here. If I go home, I still can't help my mom, and Dad can't be with me either. So I want to stay. I want to compete in the horse show in three weeks. That's what will keep me focused now."

Mrs. Finnegan added, "Andrew mentioned today that you are very smart and independent. I must tell you that you are also extremely brave. Many girls would've just frozen in your situation. I honestly don't even know what I would've done. You acted so quickly that it amazes me how you stood up to him…and drove the truck."

With a crooked smiled I asked, "Did you tell my Dad it was a stick shift? It was his idea to learn."

"Well," she said. "You must also have a very smart father."

We sat for a bit.

"I'd like you to think about one idea." Mrs. Finnegan added

"Yes?"

"When you get home, you may want to talk to a professional about what happened today to finalize it in your mind. Seeing a therapist can be very helpful after a bad experience."

"I will. I promise."

"And you will see me immediately if you have any concerns. That's important."

"Thank you, Mrs. Finnegan."

I called Dad to remind him to pick me up Friday, the fourth for my appointment with Dr. Landt. He asked, "Are you positive you want to finish the summer at camp? If you want to come home, I understand."

"That guy's in jail and I'm trying the breathing exercises Dr. Landt gave me the last time. Now I always go everywhere with someone, so I'm OK."

"You're really a force, Phoebe. Now I don't mind the front-end damage to the car when you were learning to drive the manual transmission," he laughed. "Call me if you need anything,"

We hung up when Robin walked over.

"I don't know what I'd have done if that had happened to me," she said.

"I just saw the shovel and grabbed it. I didn't even think it through. He could have used it against me if he'd been any bigger."

Robin sighed, "I never suspected that his hanging around here would turn out like that. Horrible."

"Yeah, hanging around is a good description for watching us. It was a crapshoot who he'd go after. Lucky me."

Then there was the surprise call from Andrew. I showed Robin who was calling. She motioned to talk to her later.

"Hey, Phoebe. Heard about today. I'm so sorry. Mom told me."

"I'm OK. Just shaken."

There was a slight pause before Andrew said, "Uh, I was wondering if you thought about that ride we're supposed to take."

"What do you have in mind?"

"How about Monday morning at seven? It's nice then. What do you say?"

"I say OK," and my arm shot in the air. Whoopee!

It was true that I didn't go anywhere by myself for a while after that experience. If anyone went to the showers, I'd go. Going to the pool? I'd go, too, just so I wouldn't be alone in the cabin. I hoped this anxious feeling would pass soon. The girls were really good about hanging out with me.

Sunday was a busy day. We had a big fourth week camp celebration in the afternoon with races and fun team events including an awesome pie throwing contest with whipped cream galore for Seneca and Iroquois. We really nailed the counselors. A lot of laundry was going to be picked up on Monday.

I set my alarm for six fifteen Monday morning, so I could get up to the barn at seven, and uh-oh, I forgot I had to go to the barn alone. I steeled myself to start walking toward the path, but already felt weird and uneasy. Within ten steps I was jogging, then running full blast up the hill. At the top I caught my breath and forced myself to slow down. OK, there's no problem I repeated to myself, trying to talk the panic down. Crap, I hated this anxiety thing. Andrew was there, gave me a thumbs up sign, and I nodded sheepishly.

He had Charisma saddled already, so I took Dodi out and got her set. We went out past the barn to one of the wooded trails. I had a sweatshirt because it was still cool, but I knew I'd be shedding it within a half hour. He was familiar with the paths, and I followed behind. A dozen crows joined us in the woods, cawing a warning at two hawks above. We came to a stream, probably the one Robin and I found on our way to Up The Creek. I felt the tension leaving my body listening to the soothing rhythm of muffled hoof beats in the soft earth.

We trotted forward and crossed a few meadows. There was a low two-foot fence about 150 feet away. I was completely relaxed riding Dodi with Andrew up ahead. I caught up to him and kept pace when he glanced over and said, "Let's go for it." We stayed at a trot, then cantered in a straight line toward the rail and jumped easily. We headed up a slight hill with our horses taking another fence in stride. One more easy canter later, we came to an overgrown meadow. Off to the left I saw that awful, decrepit house.

We stopped as I pointed to it and said, "Two weeks ago, that place was full of dogs. It was horrible. It's abandoned now."

"What happened to the animals?" he asked.

"I'm hoping Mrs. Tully will let me know." I told him what she did, and my spirits lifted seeing that the dogs were gone.

We turned around and did one quick race followed by a cool-down walk all the way back.

"This was a good idea. Thanks for thinking of it, Andrew. I feel so much better riding with you."

He said, "There's another trail I like we can try next time. How about Wednesday?"

"Sounds good. Let's try a few jumps again. That was good practice today."

We left the horses brushed, watered and back in their stalls for the morning group. Again, I ran down the hill to Seneca with the imagined bogeyman on my tail. I had to get my fear of being alone and those awful panic attacks under control. Maybe spending more time with Andrew would help? With him, I didn't worry.

We had three weeks to practice for the horse show. Mrs. Tully seemed to hold back her stinging critiques of me after the barn incident, but I needed to hear from her that I was slacking off. Even though I felt very confident when I was riding with Andrew, I still balked at the wall jumps. They weren't made of brick, just wood. Not barricades, I kept telling myself. I watched the other riders' body positions and hands closely to understand why I felt uneasy. The wall was just a wall to everyone else – just jump over it.

On Tuesday, Robin and I stayed behind after our lesson to help with the stalls. Mrs. Tully said she had news for us. When she sent over the photos and a report of the hoarding location to the local humane society, the action went through channels to seize the animals. The process is different by states and the police had to be involved first. She was given some information about the animals.

She said, "There were fifty-three dogs and seventeen cats. The people were evicted for health reasons, and the house had to be condemned because of the filth. The people are temporarily in a motel and claimed they were saving the dogs, not harming them. The veterinarians said otherwise. I'm glad you spoke up about it, girls. It's unthinkable to leave animals in those conditions. Hopefully, the owners will be prosecuted."

"Are there veterinarians around here to handle that many animals?" Robin asked.

"Probably not enough for all of them in this situation. Some will be sent to other locations, I imagine. This type of hoarding is a problem for any community, because there just aren't enough local resources for health checks, feed, and hopefully placing them in good homes. Huge expenses are involved."

"I hope they do find good homes after living like that," Robin said.

I met Andrew at the barn Wednesday morning. I felt better than I had all summer except for jetting up the hill away from whatever ghoul or phantom might appear from the scary woods. When he noticed that I was out of breath, he asked if I was planning on trying out for track.

"No, actually," I said. "Still thinking that Creepy Eddie is out there."

Andrew's face froze when he realized what I meant and he did something really nice. He took my shoulder and pulled me in saying, "You're safe here, and you're with me now."

OK. That's when my crush crossed over to love.

On our way to the trails we talked about our families. Andrew opened up first. "I live with my dad in Greenwich, and I usually come here for a couple of weeks in the summer."

I said, "Now that you're seventeen, doesn't your mom or dad want you to get a job?"

"I did," he answered. "There's a club in the area where I'm a lifeguard. It keeps me out of trouble all day, and I've pulled a couple of kids out of the water already. The morning is the only time I have free to ride."

"When do you go back to your dad's?"

He said, "I usually stay only part of the summer here, but with the lifeguarding, I'll go home late August just before school starts. Mom loves it here, and the camp and stable are a perfect business for her."

"Oh, good, we'll get to keep riding together until then. I usually go with Sharon, my best friend back home. I was living at her house 'cause my parents split up." I waited for a minute. "My mom had a breakdown, and she's still in the hospital."

He looked over. "I'm so sorry."

"Thanks, she's getting better."

"Will they let her out soon?"

"Whoa. That sounds like she's tied up in a padded room," I joked.

"Oops, I mean will she be home soon?"

"I hope so. Then maybe all the other stuff that's going on can get cleared up, too. I'm sure you remember the crazy girl from the park."

"Yow, sure do. Are you going to tell me about it?"

"Her mom and my dad are supposedly in love. Jackie thinks it's my mom's fault, I guess. She's been dissing my whole family about it."

"I was impressed you stood up to her."

"That's me. Fearless Phoebe," I said. "The other thing is Jackie already knew something that I didn't know. My actual birth mother was Dad's second wife. I just found out a couple of weeks ago and I blew up at everybody in my path."

"Uh, that must have been a shock."

"My mom was afraid Keira was going to take me away. It partly led to why she's in the hospital. You're the one who's made a difference in my mood, for sure."

"I think riding is how you deal with stress," Andrew said.

"It's more about who I'm riding with," as I urged Dodi into a race out to the long meadow and back.

As we came closer to the stable, I could see Frank waving at us.

"Andrew, your mom was just taken to the hospital with a broken leg. She fell off Tango over a fence."

Andrew handed off Charisma to Frank and took off running to get his car, yelling, "Gotta go, Peebes."

I finished cleaning up with Frank, and when I joined the girls at breakfast, the topic was my "date".

"It was all cool," I said. "Andrew's a great guy. Good listener, too. He had to take off for the hospital 'cause Mrs. Finnegan had a riding accident. I hope she's OK."

Andrew's concern for his mother reminded me that instead of asking more questions about Keira's life two weeks ago, I hung up on her. She had called me, so now I had to step up. Back at Seneca, I took my phone from the duffle and pressed her number, aware of the terrible pressure in my head.

She picked up on the second ring. I asked straight out, shaking as I spoke, "I'm two hours from Stamford. Can you come to meet me while I'm at summer camp?"

She paused and replied, "I think so." After a few seconds, "Possibly next week."

"Have you said anything to your kids yet?"

"No, I haven't. When the time is right, I will. Would you like to meet next Wednesday, around one?"

"OK. The directions are on the website, and it's easy to find. I'll be at the main hall after lunch," I said.

"I look forward to this, Phoebe. I've waited a long time."

I was still shaking when we hung up.

Andrew's text later said that his mom was doing well, and he asked me to go riding again. I could hardly wait to see him.

On Sunday, we walked up to the barn together and tacked up Dodi and Charisma once again.

On the trail leading out I asked how his mom was doing.

"She's amazing. She's in this huge cast but insists she doesn't want help. I've been taking her meals from the camp kitchen so she doesn't have to cook. Yesterday, in the garden, she was determined to pull weeds, so I helped her do that, or rather she directed me."

I said, "She seems so independent. That's great she's getting around." We continued up a different hilly trail that led to a beautiful view of the distant mountains.

"When your parents divorced, were you upset about choosing where you'd live?" I asked.

Andrew said, "It was so long ago. Back then it was hard for me to understand why they split up. Dad never liked it up here 'cause it wasn't convenient for his job. Mom was so into the horsey set with all her friends, and he didn't really fit in, I think. I lived here with Mom until high school. Then Dad took over. I can see you're really upset about your parents, but you'll get used to it. That I know."

"After your mom's accident, I called my birth mother, Keira, and asked if she'd drive here. I was so nervous, shaking when I was talking to her, but she said she was looking forward to seeing me. She's coming next week. I'm excited about it, but I've also gone behind Mom's back, so I feel bad."

"Since you're going through with this, I'd guess the pressure on your mom would be less. It'll already be done by the time she gets out of the hospital, and she won't worry about your being taken away, as you said."

"Ya' know, it's so strange that it's hard to talk to anyone but you about Dad and his stupid lover, and Jackie, and now my birth mom. I was completely blind to so many bombshells, and that hurt."

176

He answered, "You have to find a way to make sense of it without blaming anyone. How many events led up to what your family is going through? It's like a domino effect. One action leads to another. Mistakes are made. Then you learn to deal with the changes – or you become a Ninja and take out everyone in your path."

"The Ninja part sounds like my soon-to-be stepsister, Jackie."

"Oh, wow. That's definitely not the way to go," he said.

"My shrink tells me to chill out before reacting. After I see Dr. Landt in August and unload all my anger again, I'll be able to stick to safe subjects with my mom at the hospital. She's getting better, but some topics are nuclear."

"I'll bet you're great with her. You can make people feel good – like you do with me," he said softly as he tugged my hair.

Andrew was right that I was trying to put blame on others. I'd have to remember that for Dr. Landt's next appointment.

All through Monday and Tuesday, my mood had slipped from snappy bitch to talking non-stop about seeing Keira. Robin just rolled her eyes, and Jane remarked, "I can understand how worked up you are, but try to remember, she must have some issues, too. Bring your phone with you in case you need one of us, OK? It might get awkward."

I had my clothes picked out plus the horse necklace and Dad's birthday watch that I'd wear, the place we'd sit and talk, the subjects and questions I'd bring up. Where were her kids while she was here? I tried to picture her in my mind, looking for any resemblance. Meeting her was so distracting that Mrs. Tully was getting after me for not listening during lessons. Keira had definitely upset my ch'i.

Wednesday at breakfast I was ready. I had all my questions in mind. Everything was going to go well.

My riding group went up to our lesson and came back for lunch that I barely touched. There was no time to help at the barn today, so I waited. Disappointment sunk in as the minutes

178

ticked by. At one thirty I walked over to the pool area and watched the girls doing swim practice. No car pulled up. At two, I pressed Call and got Keira's voice mail. I knew she wasn't coming. Maybe I came on too strong. It must have been me. I scared her off.

I walked to Seneca, trying not to admit how crushing this was. Rejected again by the same woman who rejected me in the first place. I collapsed on my bed and cried. When I saw Robin and Chantel I welcomed their concern this time, as they came over to sit with me. Keira's unsaid message was clear, but the stupid little voice in my head kept saying there was a mistake. Something must have prevented her from driving here. I could see in Robin's eyes that I was kidding myself, even though she was kind enough not to say it out loud. Linda brought over a dark chocolate candy bar to ease my pain.

I could picture Dad talking about how I'd be disappointed, and he wouldn't want me to feel hurt if she didn't want to meet me. Leave it alone and don't contact her. I felt good working on this by myself. Even if it came out badly, I'd be the one deciding the next action. With Drew coming in two days to drive me back home for the weekend, there was no rescheduling anything now. Another meeting would have to wait.

Friday afternoon, Drew was coming from his girlfriends' house in Millerton to avoid having to drive up and back to

Maple Ridge on the same day. Andrew had already left for lifeguarding, so their meet and greet would have to wait till another time.

Traffic was heavy going back home adding additional time to the trip. When we pulled up to the garage, I said, "Wait, Drew, I have to tell you something before we go inside. Keira promised to come to see me and didn't show up."

Shocked, he said, "You made plans to meet her?"

"Yes. She said she was looking forward to it. But I guess not enough to call and tell me she wouldn't be there."

"I am so sorry. Maybe that's why Dad and Patrice kept her away. Maybe she's unreliable."

"Don't tell Dad, OK? I wanted to do something for myself, and it didn't work out too well," I said.

"Next time, call me. Every once in a while, I can be of help."

"Are you kidding me? This summer would have been a total bust without you, Drew."

Dad called to us from the front door and said, "What's the hold up you two? Come inside. Dinner's ready."

We ate barbeque in the kitchen talking about what to expect Saturday at the hospital. I showed Dad and Drew some new drawings and the scented soap from Up The Creek store I would give to Mom.

Drew said, "I have some good news. I applied for a medical technology position starting in September with a New York City company. Maybe an offer is coming after the second interview next week."

Dad was pleased and said, "I'll keep covering your rent, since your mother is still on the warpath about you. What the heck did you do, anyway?"

"Her list is too long to comment on. I'll just say there was a recent incident at home with a few of my frat brothers."

Dad looked at Drew sharply, "Does it involve a bill I received for repairs to the Greenwich house?"

Drew cleared his plate quickly. "Maybe," he mumbled, and left the kitchen.

Dad said, "Phoebe, did Patrice say anything about this deposit?" He showed me the account statement. I was surprised to see $9,000 dollars recently added to her checking account. "I need you to ask your mother about this. There's a problem."

"What is it, Dad?"

"I'm not sure, I just need to find out if this is her active account. Please see what she says tomorrow."

"Uh, Dad. I know you don't want to hear this, but Mom was positive that Barbara was trying to do something to her. She said that she was talking to people to get her fired."

"I wouldn't take anything seriously from your mother right now."

"Dad, I'm just sayin'. Please check on it at Family Assistance. What's going on there?"

On the trip to White Plains to see Mom in the morning, I was pretty low. I said to Drew, "I wish I could ask Mom about Keira. She must know something about her."

Drew was quiet for a minute.

"Phoebes, this birth bomb news just reminded me of your fear of walls this summer. Keira has suddenly become this destructive block to focus on. You've hit a wall. You could easily ride over a dozen fences on your trusted Kahlua because you are confident you can do it. Then you come upon a wall that's impassable, unsolvable, impossible to surmount, making you feel like you've failed.

"Just step back, and look at it in a new perspective, and ta-da! It's just a different experience for you. So when you're trying to fix a problem ask, 'Is this a fence, or is it a wall?' You know that the fences are easy. You and Kahlua just sail right over them. Try asking why you think you're not good enough for the wall jump…or good enough for Keira.

"Don't be overcome by a challenge. Make it a challenge to overcome. Trust yourself. Rely on all you've learned growing up. That's how you'll succeed without beating yourself up in the process."

We drove to the hospital while I thought about what he said. Fences and walls. Drew was right. Keira Tierney did not define who I was. Her broken promises defines who she is.

Drew and I walked into Dr. Gordon's office.

"I'll begin with the positive," he said. "Mrs. Spring is responding to the medication nicely, but it's important at this stage that she remain on it consistently, so that adjustments can be made if necessary. However, she is fixated on a relationship between a former friend of hers and your father. This is a concern and it is being discussed at length with her during her therapy sessions."

Drew said, "Yes, we're aware of it, and we avoid bringing it up."

"At this point, that's what I would recommend. Her treatment involves being able to move forward from past negative events by concentrating on positive future goals."

Mom stood up to greet us as Drew and I followed the nurse to the community area. She was uplifted to see us. I noted that her eyes were more focused than her vacant stare of a month ago, but her conversation still bounced around different subjects.

"Thank you, Drew, for driving Phoebe to see me." She looked to me, "Sweetie, I've missed your birthday, and I've missed you so much. I saved all your letters, and they give me hope that I'll be able to go home soon."

"See? I'm wearing my birthday horse charm you sent. I found the gold chain that you gave me last year." She looked at it and smiled.

"Do you remember your camp experience, Mom? I know I will forever."

"My riding camp was in Pennsylvania, near Reading. I made friends there but haven't heard from them in years. It was one of my best childhood experiences." She paused, "I still remember how I begged my parents to buy Porsche for me, but we lived in the city then, so we couldn't."

We traded some memories of our trips to New York, Disneyworld, and out West a few years ago.

I said, "I'll come tomorrow morning before I go back to Massachusetts. I almost forgot. This letter came the other day, and I have to tell the bank if this is your account. Do you remember depositing this?"

She looked at the letter and seemed confused. "I thought I was overdrawn." When she looked at the number she said, "This can't be right."

"OK, Mom. I'll take care of it."

She nodded as we let our hug go.

Dad was waiting at home to take me to Dr. Landt's appointment. A pile of newspapers was stacked in the kitchen. I noticed a column headline that said "Family Assistance Fraud Investigation." Dad came in as I was reading the article about missing funds at the organization. I looked at Dad saying, "Do you know what this is about? Doesn't Mom do the accounting there?"

"Yes, she does, or did. What did you find out from Patrice about that account information?"

"She didn't know anything about it."

Dad looked again at the statement. "Yes, there seems to be a mistake here."

I went to my room and dialed Sharon.

She answered, "Phoebe, I'm glad you called. I talked to Asia, and Jackie knew when you were going to be at the park. She wanted to make a scene."

Jackie again, showing her ugly side. "She's really out to ruin me. I'll have to call you back. Gotta leave for Dr. Landt's now."

Sharon said, "Don't worry, we'll talk later." We hung up.

Dad dropped me at Dr. Landt's office.

I began my session with my news of the discovery of my birth mother. "After I found the birth certificate, I called her. I had questions for the woman all prepared, but she didn't come to meet me at camp on Wednesday like she promised, and Drew said something today that made sense."

"Are you saying you contacted the woman yourself?"

I admitted, "I've been withheld from so many decisions. I didn't want to wait for permission to find my own birth mother, so yes. I did it myself. She promised to drive to camp and didn't show up. I had everything planned. It was horrible."

"And your brother helped you to deal with this?"

"He said to look at my disappointments as a challenge instead of being sad about them. I know how great my mom is, and Dad used to be, because of all the experiences I've been able to have. But I'm still so angry with Dad because of the other woman he chose, Mrs. Lorrenze. Dad gave me this great camp experience, so the whole summer I was having a good time while Mom's locked up. All I could do is visit and talk with the doctor. I couldn't make any decisions or help."

"Don't you think that is why your father wanted you to enjoy the summer? He knows how you worry about her."

I was quiet for a moment.

"Also something else happened at camp. I was attacked by a worker at the stable, but I got away by stealing a camp truck. I wasn't hurt, and he got caught, but I've been really shook up, and I've been having some bad dreams. Dad wanted me to talk to you about it." Dr. Landt saw that I was shaking and handed me some tissues.

"I'm so sorry you had such a terrible experience. I've noticed that you don't wait for things to happen to you, Phoebe. When something is wrong, you don't shy away or curl up. You act. That's impressive. You have an inner strength that many adults don't have. That should be your focus. Not what could have happened, but your reaction that led you to get away from him."

"I'll try. And I kept doing my breathing exercises. It helped a little."

"Since you've come such a long way in expressing yourself, I'd like to give you this notebook to start your journal. You can write down things that make you happy or form an impression, good or bad. You're an artist, so draw some images in there as well. Whatever you're feeling, put it on paper."

Dr. Landt closed with, "You're in good hands, Phoebe, with all the people who are supporting you in this difficult situation. You'll come to see that your greatest concerns are manageable."

When Dad picked me up, I said, "I think Dr. Landt's helpful, and I made an appointment for August 24."

He said, "If you want me to go to any of the sessions, I will, you know."

I couldn't help clenching my hands. I remembered he had said that before.

I was so happy to see Sharon. Dad dropped me at her house while he did some errands. Probably to go see Mrs. Lorrenze.

I pulled out the letter and waited while Sharon read it. She looked up and said, "I'm surprised you had the nerve to call her. She writes she wants to meet you, but doesn't show up when you set it up. Doesn't make much sense. Does your dad know you spoke to her?"

"You know, he keeps everything from me. He's made a lot of un-kept promises. Now I'm just gonna do what I think is right."

We took Jasmine outside while we covered Sharon's trip to Grams, her Dad's wedding, and my Six Flags adventure all caught in technicolor on our phones.

"Wow, Andrew is really good looking," she said.

"The best part is that he listens," was my reply.

Dad picked me up for dinner, but talking was unbelievably awkward. I appreciated that he was home again and making an effort for me, but I couldn't help feeling he'd locked me out of his life. Any talk about Barbara became a war of words, and I wasn't going to mention Keira either. So we turned in early.

After breakfast on Sunday, Dad drove me to the hospital but waited in the car. The community area was busy, and Mom was talking with someone when I came over. She introduced me to Gina, another resident, before we found a spot to talk together.

Mom said, "I want Charles to spend more time with you. It's upsetting that he's always got an excuse. And now that he's with…her, I imagine you see him even less than before."

"He's been trying, Mom."

"I don't like seeing you ignored by him."

I lied. "He talked to me today about doing some things together." Changing the subject, I said, "I hope you're planning on working again. You were so into your job. It meant so much to you."

She hesitated. "If they'll let me. Barbara's meddling caused so many problems. For months she went behind my back at work. I didn't find out till just before all this," as she waved her arm around.

I switched over to the August plans. "There are only two weeks left of camp. When I get home, I can see you more often, and pretty soon you'll be home."

She said, "Time's hard to judge when you're looking at four walls."

We hugged, and there was a difference in the way she reacted to my leaving. No tears this time.

CHAPTER 15   BELIEVE

Dad and I left for Massachusetts directly from the hospital.

He opened with, "Are you sure you're OK with camp, Phoebe? You know, since the barn incident?"

"Yes, Dad, thanks for asking, but I'm OK. My friend Andrew goes with me to the barn. He's been very helpful."

I was not all right with Jackie's interference and harassment, though. I couldn't bring that up while he was driving. Would Dad believe me anyway? And take my word against what his "girlfriend" told him? I practiced instead on my calming exercises, because I could feel an eruption in the works.

We arrived in time to give Dad a tour and meet with Mrs. Finnegan to thank her for her kindness in dealing with Creepy guy. She was doing well in her cast but wouldn't be riding for a few weeks. Walking back to the car, I finally had Dad's attention. It was time to bring up Jackie.

"Coming to the camp this summer actually helped me get through Mom's illness, and thank you for insisting. Even though the trip to Six Flags could have been a disaster, I was with all these nice girls who care about me and each other."

"What do you mean a disaster? You said it was terrific," he said.

"Jackie nearly attacked me at the amusement park, Dad. She knew I was going to be there that Thursday. You need to know that Jackie finds out where I am and what I'm doing. I believe that your beloved Barbara is a mouthpiece to her, and I don't like it."

"Don't be ridiculous, Phoebe. I already spoke to her about her callousness in talking about your birth mother. Our personal information is none of her business."

"Well, there's a lot more going on than that. Did you know she painted Psycho Mom on the side of the house? And what about the horrible messages she's been leaving for me on my phone? Why are you blind to this? You can talk to Sharon, and she'll tell you the same thing."

"I'll look into what you're saying, but I think you're exaggerating."

"No. You're wearing blinkers, Dad. You've got tunnel vision. You can't see what's going on around you, and it's driving me crazy."

Silence.

"Bye, Dad. I'm sorry you don't believe me."

He raised his arms to the side and walked to the car in frustration.

Robin and the girls were talking quietly at Seneca, waiting for me to join in the conversation.

I threw my duffle on the bed and sat down hard. I thought of what Andrew told me about blaming others, but how could my father be so blind? Jane sat on Robin's bed and asked, "What happened?"

I whined, "Why can't he believe what I'm telling him?"

"You mean your dad?" asked Robin.

"He's the problem. He started it. How can he possibly help his wife when he's picked her best friend to be with? Mom wants me to be with Dad more. What is she thinking will happen?"

I grabbed a tissue, and Robin put her arm around me.

I spent most of the night watching my clock change hours until the bell sounded at eight.

With one week left till the horse show, the riders were psyched for the events. We were all busy polishing our black field boots, making sure our breeches were clean and our whites were washed and hung up to dry. Pam's dress shirt needed an exorcism after she found it squished, twisted and flattened at the bottom of her trunk.

The morning practice lessons went well on the flatwork. When it was time for the jumps, Pam was the first called in to do the course as Robin, Susan, Jane, and I waited outside the ring. Mrs. Tully was critiquing Pam's position, calling for more weight in her heels.

She called out, "Don't rush him," as Rowdy crowded an oxer a little too closely, then came up to a vertical, but veered off suddenly to the right leaving Pam mid air for a second before thumping to the ground on her hip.

"Oh, that was a good one!" Pam said laughing hard as she stood up and dusted herself off. Rowdy must have felt pretty feisty because he decided to go solo around the course, clearing each fence elegantly with a few bucks, kicks, and farts for emphasis.

Mrs. Tully congratulated her after making sure she was OK. "When you get dumped off, you own that spot where you fell," she announced.

Rowdy finally gave up running around when Mrs. Tully flagged him down and caught the reins. Pam and Rowdy performed their re-do very well together with Pam's fist pumping in the air after the final jump.

I noticed Andrew walking up to the ring as I waited to be called. Kahlua was alert and ready for his turn. Mrs. Tully indicated where the change of direction would be, and I started off. I'm not sure why, but I hesitated on the line to a wall causing Kahlua to avoid it, and we had to do the required circle to complete the jump. I knew this was not Kahlua's problem. It was mine.

Mrs. Tully did not scold, but just said, "You can correct this by remembering to look directly at the spot where you intend to jump."

That's what Doris told me last month. Then I focused on what Drew told me, and I looked at the wall height and not the solid base. Just a different perspective. The second time around I did it perfectly and gave Kahlua a pat on the neck. Mrs. Tully directed, "Now circle around and do exactly that again. Stop second-guessing. You're too talented to let this get to you."

Andrew was still waiting when our lesson ended and came over to walk with me as we cooled the horses down. The girls went back to Seneca while Andrew and I stood at the ring. "I think you've got it, Peebes. Now you'll wonder why it was ever a problem."

"Fences to me have always been easy. I've fallen off before, but I'd never been afraid of them. I had psyched myself out about the walls, but Drew explained to me how to get over that. Literally," I laughed.

Andrew pulled me into a hug and kissed me. "Whatever you do, you still look great, either on or off the saddle."

I didn't care if anyone was watching when I kissed him back.

For Susan's fourteenth birthday on Tuesday, we serenaded her loudly while walking up to the barn. We made a first place ribbon for Secret and her, placing it on his bridle as she led him to the ring. She laughed at the gesture, while she gave Secret a nice pat before mounting up. She was quickly alarmed to find his gait was off and immediately dismounted to check him over. Frank looked at Secret's front legs and hooves and figured it may be an abscess. The vet was called in that afternoon and confirmed it. Dr. Hood drained the abscess and applied a poultice, telling Frank to apply additional wraps that would help clear it. It could take up to two weeks to heal. Susan was very upset because she had hinted that she wanted her parents to purchase him once the summer was over, and the injury prevented her from riding Secret until he was sound. We could see her disappointment and said we'd help her figure out which horse she'd ride during the final practices and the show on Saturday. Bummer of a birthday.

That night at dinner, we all went over to the Iroquois table and gave Susan a card from Seneca just as the cake and ice cream came. I had drawn a cartoon of a huge lopsided cake topped with fourteen horses facing different directions in silly jumping positions. The caption read, "Jump for Joy on your Birthday. Love, the Seneca Crew" with all our names. She smiled and held it up.

The rain on Wednesday morning interrupted the first part of our lesson, but we were able to complete the second half. Susan went right to Secret's stall to check on him while Frank was applying another poultice. We saddled our horses while Mrs. Tully led a gorgeous 16.0 Hanoverian for Susan to ride. She said, "This is Tango, Mrs. Finnegan's own horse, and she's happy to let you train on him for the show. I might have mentioned to her how talented a rider you are." Susan was speechless at first, but managed to thank Mrs. Tully for her help.

Mrs. Tully waved us into the center. "All right, ladies. We're going to try a different exercise today. The five of you gather together in a line, do a sitting trot to the far end of the ring. Three go left and two go right and change to a posting trot. Then, Susan will split off and canter diagonally across to join the left-side group. At the top of the ring, join together, repeat the five abroad with Pam splitting off and cantering diagonally across to the other side." It was a nice break from the usual flat work. We still had time to practice two courses over fences, and Susan found Tango to be a dream.

We finished walking the horses out and let them graze as the sky began to cloud over. The minute the rain and distant thunder started, Mrs. Tully yelled to us to get them to the barn. Lightning cracked to the ground, and another strike speared a large oak tree causing a branch to smoke and land next to the tractor barn. Mrs. Tully ran to the hose and turned it on full blast as Frank doused the smoking ember. The horses were spooked as we secured the doors to their stalls, but we quickly left to help outside. Jane was in the lead when another broken branch fell almost hitting her. Frank made sure that the fire was extinguished, and we all took cover at the barn entrance watching the deluge. Huge raindrops pummeled the dirt driveway creating big puddles in the ruts. We stood at the open doorway and took in that strong fresh air smell and humid breeze that always accompanies summer downpours as the storm slowly died down. We patted our heads dry with some towels and ventured back out to check the other barn. Frank cleared away the branch and noted that damage was limited only to the outside barn wall.

On our way back to Seneca, Pam said, "Well, that was some storm. We should bring a little excitement back to Seneca."

Jane said, "We could short sheet the other girls' beds while they're still out."

It's a dumb trick, but usually gets a laugh. Well, usually, but not that night. They were so pissed at us. I had to bribe them for forgiveness with candy my Dad sent. Then we were OK.

I had been writing in my journal every day since seeing Dr. Landt. I was putting so many thoughts to paper I was going to run out of pages before the summer ended. After writing, "To hell with being afraid, just get the jump done," I drew myself flying over a wall and Kahlua jumping after me, remembering Drew's words about accepting challenges.

I also liked jotting down a quick impression, or a sketched face with the different moods I experienced during the day. I cut out one article on "Great Moms" from a magazine and tucked that into my book. I took notes and found that everything in it outlined how much Mom did for me even when I did something stupid. We would laugh about the dumbest things together.

I've always felt bad for people who couldn't understand humor. Did they perhaps fear that people were laughing at them? One time I was walking through town with three other girls but not looking ahead to where I was going. I was talking to the girl on my left and smacked my body straight into a telephone pole. Like how could I possibly miss seeing this huge obstacle? It felt good to laugh at myself with the other girls, even though it was embarrassing.

In my next letter to Mom I told her that I wore the horse charm every day and thought of her being home to greet me after camp. It was a simple sentence, but it was the most positive thought I could send to her. The letter had a few sketches of riders and the barn that Mom would like. I read it over, then folded it in the envelope ready for an address.

I had put the hurt of Keira not showing up out of my mind when I saw there was a message on my phone from her. I thought about deleting it, but the impulse to check it was too hard to ignore. "This is Keira. I apologize for not coming, Phoebe. I was ready to go, but was called in to my job, so I couldn't make it. We'll try for another day when you want."

Should I trust her to try again? Finding out more about her was so close to happening. I felt that I had to give her another chance. I didn't want her there for the horse show, so it would have to be next week. I texted back, "I was sorry, too, that you didn't let me know. I would like to see you on Wednesday. Please text if you can come." Her text came back with, "Yes, see you at one." I didn't want to get so worked up this time, and thankfully I had a lot going on between now and then.

Saturday arrived, and we were ready for our big camp event. Andrew came to the barn early to wish me luck but had to work and couldn't stay. A lot of parents had their cameras and video cams in hand waiting patiently for their girls to show off their horsemanship skills. The equestrians had signed up to enter both the flat and jumper classes in the afternoon. We watched most of the morning classes while cheering the younger kids on.

It was a great afternoon for me because I was cautiously optimistic that Dad's appearance showed he was making an effort this time. Drew, Dad, and I stood at the rails together drinking lots of water to beat the heat until it was time to compete. Our flat class went very well. The judge awarded me first, Susan second, and Jane third place. We were pretty competitive, but it was in good fun.

The jumping class results went a bit differently. I sailed over the oxers, coup, verticals, and was determined to complete both walls on the first try. Kahlua and I finished our round with one fault. I looked at Drew and nodded, and he gave a thumbs up. Susan had a perfect run on Tango for her first place, I received second, and Pam took third. Susan was also excited about hearing Mrs. Finnegan's news that Secret's abscess was healing. Dr. Hood was coming Monday for a recheck.

After the show, a barbeque was set up outside where some of the dads were helping out at the grills. As we sat down to eat, I laughed noticing many of the camp girls' googly-eyed expressions and O shaped mouths silently saying, "Holy cow, that's your brother?"

Mom's progress during the past week started the conversation. Dad said that Dr. Gordon's prediction was correct regarding the medication adjustment, and thought she might be able to go home within two weeks. I was really surprised and glad it would be that soon.

There was a long silence before he started to speak about Mrs. Lorrenze. I almost plugged my ears, but decided I'd give him a minute to talk.

"I think you need to hear this, Phoebe. Barbara came to me a few months back, concerned about Patrice's behavior at

Family Assistance. She was demanding too much of the volunteers and actually several people left when no one could reason with her. I had no intention of starting anything, but Barbara was also going through difficulty at home, and we talked about having similar issues. We did start seeing each other then, and I'm not sure how Patrice found out."

I said, "Dad, you also left Darleen for another woman."

He made no response.

"And you left Drew behind when you met Keira. He didn't see you the whole time you were with Keira." I looked at Drew and he nodded.

Dad countered, "I wasn't married when I met Patrice. My marriage to Keira was over almost when it started. I explained to you already about Keira's gambling."

"So you and Barbara are all lovey dovey now, and Jackie's getting a free pass for whatever she wants to do or say about me? Did you tell Barbara what Jackie's doing?"

"I spoke to Jackie myself, and she insists otherwise. I do believe all these issues you are both having are certainly valid, but if we can talk about it, before it gets blown out of proportion, everything can be resolved. I promise you."

"Jackie said that I was spending money I don't have. Are we broke or something?"

"No. I don't know why she'd say that."

I felt so sad about Dad's being OK with Barbara and Jackie's negative impact on my life. Like termites, burrowing in where they don't belong, they were eating up my home life until there was nothing left.

The camp announcements followed the barbeque dinner, and our conversation was interrupted.

With one week left to our camp experience, Mrs. Finnegan thanked the counselors, trainers, and the rest of the staff for their dedication. She also thanked the campers for their efforts in making the summer so enjoyable. She hoped our experience would remain in our memories for many years and invited us to return the following year. We picked up plates of watermelon to finish off the show day.

When Mrs. Finnegan saw Dad, he got up to talk with her. I had my chance to speak with Drew privately. "I wish that Dad would believe me about Barbara. There's something wrong with that woman, I'm sure of it, and Keira called me back. She's coming on Wednesday. I know you're skeptical, but I think she'll be here this time."

Drew wasn't optimistic. "I know how trusting you are, Phoebe. I just don't want you to think it means anything if she blows off this meeting, too. I imagine it's a big step even for her to see the daughter she's missed all these years. I hope she does get to meet you, because she'll understand the mistake she made."

"I'll be fine. She said she'd come, and I'd rather do this now than wonder about it forever," I said smiling.

Drew gave me a hug before the three of us walked to the car. Dad pulled a package from the back and handed it to me. When I opened it, there was a delicate stained glass horse sculpture that I could hang in front of a window to allow the light to glimmer through it. He said, "I remember how much you love the windows at the church. This just reminded me of the colors there. I'll bring this back for you today if you'd like."

I started to cry just as they were leaving. I just wanted to ask why he couldn't move back home, but I couldn't get the words out. I choked out, "OK. Thanks, it's so pretty, I wouldn't want it to be broken," but Drew saw my reaction, knowing how left out of Dad's life I was feeling.

Drew pulled me into a hug and patted my head saying, "Not to worry, kiddo."

And they drove away.

Monday it rained again after our lesson but not like the deluge of the week before. We finished up just as the drizzle started and helped Frank mucking the stalls. We were back in Seneca when Chantel received a call from home. She had to pack up the next day because her Mom and Dad were going on a business trip and couldn't pick her up on Saturday. We got her in a silly mood to distract her from having to leave camp early.

Her birthday was on Friday, so Robin and Linda went to the dining hall to arrange for a surprise cake for her.

She was bummed out through dinner, but when the cake and sixteen candles came out, the look on Chantel's face was priceless. She was so happy that we remembered. The girls all signed a card that I had made, showing her falling off Dominic, which had happened the week before the show. It said, "You're not considered a rider until your horse gives you at least one alternate dismount." Robin presented her with a horseshoe decorated with a huge bow and a giant Hershey bar to remember us.

She exploded with laughter and said, "Now I can think of myself as an equestrian," as she got up and hugged every one of us at Seneca.

Our group had a really good Tuesday morning. After our lesson, I changed and walked to the pool with Jane. We were doing laps when Andrew came by and sat to watch us. I swam over to the side to say hi.

"Are you done swimming soon? Would you like to go for a walk?" Andrew asked.

Jane had said earlier that she was going to archery in the afternoon, so I agreed to meet Andrew at the dining hall later.

He said, "I want to show you something." I followed him past the large fenced garden from where the camp's fresh vegetables were grown. Andrew continued toward a column of slender Thuja evergreens to a narrow pathway. I was so surprised when we came upon a beautiful hidden garden amidst the tall trees.

I said, "Andrew. I never knew this was even here. This is so pretty."

We walked around the space taking in the selection of roses, astilbe, and geraniums spaced colorfully around areas of coleus, petunias, and impatiens. The tall ornamental grasses gave the place a soft and airy look. It was so peaceful and seemed far away from a busy camp. A crunchy stone pathway curved toward the center where I saw a bronze plaque on the ground that read, "Brooke's garden".

I stood next to Andrew and asked quietly, "Who is Brooke?"

"She was my older sister. She was killed in a car accident two years ago."

I said, "Oh, I'm so sorry."

"Mom especially took it very hard. She loves gardening and spends a lot of time working here. She started it right after Brook died."

"It's so peaceful. Thank you for sharing this," I said.

"I don't bring everyone here. Just people who I think will appreciate it."

"I won't forget it," I added.

We strolled back toward the pool and sat in a couple of chairs watching some of the girls finish their swim routine. I thought about having only a few more days of being here. Andrew's attention to my problems had minimized my negative attitude toward Dad and his new life with Barbara, but Mom was going to need me so much.

He caught me by surprise saying, "I think we should get together after summer vacation. What do you think about going riding at your stable?"

I could ask Andrew anything, and he wouldn't think it silly or meaningless. He could talk me through any problem, like it was no more worry than a hangnail, but Mom had to be my first concern when I was home.

I said, "We'll have so much fun on the trails. But I need to make sure my mom is OK and home to stay."

"That sounds like a plan."

He walked me back toward the cabin path, and we decided to meet every morning for the rest of the week for our final rides and walks together. No subject seemed to be off limits, and sometimes being quiet was enough. That evening, I wrote to my mom about Andrew in one of my last letters from camp.

"Dear Mom,

Thank you for being my Mom. This summer went by very quickly for me, though I imagine for you it did not. When you come home, we'll go to your favorite places, like the Met in the city to make up for the time we lost together. Can't wait! I wish you could see the camp, but I have plenty of photos for you.

Also, so you won't be surprised, I met a boy named Andrew, and he's the owner's son. He'll be visiting us in the fall, and I know you'll like him.

I think about you every day.

I miss you! PS"

Wednesday morning, Andrew and I spent quite awhile cuddling in one of the meadows as I talked about seeing Keira later. We made plans for riding at Maple Hill, which made our last few days together a breeze, because I knew he'd come to see me soon.

I was pretty upbeat during my morning lesson, having gone through the mental process of getting ready for Keira's visit. I was positive she wouldn't let this go by. The girls and I went to lunch and this time insisted on staying with me at the dining hall until she was supposed to arrive. As the minutes clicked away, pretty soon I knew it was going to be a repeat of last Wednesday. This time, I wasn't waiting more than I had to, so after a half hour, I grabbed Robin's arm and said, "Let's go. We have better things to do."

They tried to liven up the rest of the day with a swim at the pool, but I was pretty quiet. No matter how I tried, I couldn't figure out what I'd done wrong. Why wasn't she interested? I don't even live that far away. She could have come forward sooner than a year ago. I had to forget about her. She was, as Drew said, unreliable.

The girls were busy during the final days organizing their trunks, getting addresses and numbers into their cell phones, and making plans for future get-togethers. I thought it would be fun to have a reunion of the five equestrians, but I knew I wouldn't be able to host it right away. Maybe one of the others would step up to arrange a riding day.

On Saturday morning, the seven of us from Seneca did a group hug and chatted till our families came to claim us. I still wasn't sure whether Drew or Dad would be coming for me. I was waiting in the dining hall when Linda came over.

"Phoebe, this is my mom."

"Hi, Mrs. Bonner," shaking her hand politely.

"Linda sent many letters saying how kind you and the other girls have been, about getting her interested in riding."

"Linda did that on her own. She liked it as soon as she tried it."

"That's what I mean," Mrs. Bonner said. "Linda wasn't interested in trying anything before. You and the other girls completely changed that. She wants to continue lessons."

"Is there a stable near your home where you can go?" I asked Linda.

"They've already checked out two of them for me."

I looked at my campmate. "Glad it worked out for you this summer. We had kind of a bumpy start," I smiled.

"But you made the difference, and I want to come back next summer," she said.

I turned when I saw Drew. "Have a good year, Linda, and I might be back next summer, too. My brother just got here, so I have to go. Nice to meet you, Mrs. Bonner."

"Phoebe, it was great to meet you. And thank you."

I watched the raised eyebrow looks from the girls as well as some of the moms, when Drew walked through the doorway. Amazing what he could do to a room full of women!

"Do you want some coffee?" I asked him. "It's freshly brewed."

He took a cup and looked around.

"How are you doing on this last day?" he asked.

"Sad. This was the worst, best summer, and I'm definitely going to miss everything and everybody here."

"Would you like to go up to the barn one last time?" he asked.

"I was hoping you'd go with me," I answered, grabbing his arm.

Drew stopped at the car and pulled two envelopes out. We came to the top of the hill in time to see Mrs. Tully pull up in her truck. Frank was in the barn, and we joined them.

Drew handed over the cards to each and said, "This is to thank you for taking such good care of this one. It's from our dad."

We talked as the four of us walked through the aisle greeting each horse by name. When we got to Secret Victory's stall, I gave him a pat, disturbing the chicken that sat on his rump.

"How's he doing now?" I asked Frank.

"Susan's going to be happy. Mr. Fisk showed an interest in buying him once the abscess is gone. He'll be vetted, and hopefully he'll be on his way to new digs soon. Looks like Jane may purchase Felix also. He's a great horse, too, very fit," he said.

I got teary when we arrived at Kahlua's place and watched him eating hay. Mrs. Tully gave me a big carrot from her pocket. I palmed it and gave it to him.

Mrs. Tully said, "They're still going to be here next summer if you decide to return. Mrs. Finnegan is an avid rider, and the farm continues as a stable all year. Some camps don't keep all of their horses as we do. I hope you go to some of the sanctioned shows in your area. You have a lot of talent, Phoebe."

"This was a great experience for me, and if Dad says yes, I'd like to come back. I have one more year till I'm sixteen."

We said goodbye, and walked back down the hill to get my things.

Drew drove the car to the cabin to load up when I said, "I really want to say goodbye to Andrew and Mrs. Finnegan."

"OK. Dad has cards and checks for Brianna and Martina."

I looked around at the sun-lit paths and lawn while we drove back to the dining hall. Mrs. Finnegan was standing in front of the office speaking with other parents but waved when she saw Drew and me.

She greeted me as we walked over. "Andrew is working today at the pool, but I understand that he's looking forward to seeing you in the fall, so don't be a stranger, Phoebe."

Wow. Andrew had told her about our plans.

"Thank you, Mrs. Finnegan. I hope he can come visit me in New York."

We waved, buckled into the Audi and drove off.

We took a scenic route because it was such a nice day. Drew wanted to stop at a little café in Millerton, NY, for a late lunch. Drew waved to a girl at a table by the window when we walked in. He introduced me to Emily Bartlett as he gave her a kiss on the cheek.

He said, "Emily lives near here. We went to Lehigh together, and she has one year left before graduating."

Emily Bartlett was a very pretty, tanned, and athletic girl with long, wavy blond hair. I noticed when she stood up at the front display case to place our sandwich order, that she was almost as tall as Drew. The three of us checked out the assortment of homemade baked goods and selected a few while waiting for the sandwiches to be ready.

Back at our table Emily said, "Phoebe, I heard that you had an exciting summer in Massachusetts and that you are very talented on horseback."

"I had a good trainer. She helped me a lot. Drew rides, too."

Emily had a summer job working at a local shop. She said her father was a respected sculptor and her parents left the city to allow him to work in a quiet setting.

I asked, "What's the program you're studying?"

"I love Lehigh. I'm doing the secondary ed program with one more year till graduation. Then hopefully, I'll be employed and pay off my student loan."

"Where will you be looking for a job?" I asked.

"In New York, but I'm open."

Drew said, "Emily's had some of her short stories published in a few magazines. I can send you a link to a couple of them."

She added, "I've always been interested in historical events and came up with a couple of fictional characters that are included in the plots."

"I'd like to read a couple. Sounds interesting. Anything in art, since your father's an artist?" I asked.

"I have one in the works now, with some kinks to iron out. When it's done, I'll be sure to send you a copy."

We finished lunch and took a slow walk around town. I climbed in the Audi while Emily leaned into the car for a wistful kiss from Drew. She waved as we pulled away.

Thinking of Andrew, I asked, "Is it tough to have a long distance relationship?"

"We were dating for over a year at Lehigh. Now I won't be able to see her every weekend. Yes, it's going to be hard, but she's worth it."

We drove back to my house for the night, so I could unpack my trunk and put clothes in the laundry. I knew the fridge was going to be empty, so we stopped for takeout on the way home.

Drew said during dinner, "I've been thinking about your experience with your birth mom. There's going to be a lot going on in the next week with Patrice coming home, so you may want to put Keira on the back burner for awhile."

"She's already done that for me with her second no-show. It's hurtful," I said.

"Just know you can call me. OK?"

After clearing the dishes, I sorted the mail and set aside Mom's current bank statement showing the amount Dad questioned, $9,000.

On Sunday, Drew dropped me off at Sharon's with clothes I'd need for a week. Andrew had already texted me, and I called him back on his cell before dinner. He said, "Wish I'd gotten to say goodbye. I'll be in Greenwich next week. How's your mom doing?"

I replied, "I think, better. I'm staying at Sharon's, but I want to go back home. Once Mom's home, I hope you can come to meet everybody."

"That can't be soon enough for me," he said.

We signed off and I went upstairs.

I asked Sharon, "Is it different now that your Dad's married again?"

"Well, I'm uncomfortable at their house. I wish I didn't feel that way, but it's like being left out. It wasn't like that before this summer, so I can't figure why it's not the same."

"With how Jackie is acting toward me, I'll probably never want to see Dad again," I said as I got upset.

Sharon added, "But Jackie's living with her dad now, anyway. Best case, you'll see him alone without Barbara or Jackie."

Sharon and I were eating breakfast Monday morning when Dad called asking if I could go over to the house soon and sort through the mail.

I asked, "Did you call the bank about Mom's account? There's a new statement on the desk I found Saturday."

"I spoke with the manager yesterday. He's going to look into it."

"And don't forget, please, you promised to take me on Thursday to see Dr. Landt."

215

We cleaned the plates and took Jasmine outside.

Sharon said, "Mom just called and wanted to know if we wanted to go to the mall in Fairbury. Would you like to go today?"

I was still burning about Dad not believing me about Jackie. Maybe it would help to be distracted.

Mrs. Sinks came back to pick us up for the shopping trip. It was a sunny day, and during the week the mall wouldn't be so crowded. We liked Fairbury because of the medium to upscale stores and good places to eat.

Our first stop was J.Jill where I found two cute tops. Both Mrs. Sinks and Sharon bought shorts. At Foot Locker I was able to buy sneakers I needed after the muck at the camp. We decided to skip the food court and went to the Cheesecake Factory for lunch with Sharon's mom treating us. We stopped at the Apple Store to check out the new phones before finding some nice gifts at Bath & Body for Mrs. Sinks and my mom. Haagen-Dazs had my favorite Belgian chocolate ice cream that I polished off before we ended up wandering around Macy's shoe department. Then, holy crap, there was Jackie. I turned away, but it was too late. She spotted me.

She screamed, "You're going to be doing a lot of explaining when the cops come to your house and start asking questions." She took a shoe from the display and threw it at me.

I glanced at Mrs. Sinks who was horrified. I'm not sure if she really believed me before, but Jackie's raving outburst left nothing to the imagination. The salespeople were watching in shock. Sharon practically dragged me toward the exit with Mrs. Sinks catching up.

I could hear Jackie yelling, "Your mom's going to pay for what she did!" as we escaped.

"Now I get what you've been going through," Mrs. Sinks offered.

"And when will it stop?" I asked.

I thanked Mrs. Sinks for the shopping trip when we were back at her house. I picked up their newspaper and took it into the kitchen while glancing at another article on the misplacement of funds at Family Assistance. An outside audit was being conducted.

Drew, not Dad, came back again on Thursday morning to take me to Dr. Landt's. During the session, I shared several paragraphs in my journal about my strong feelings toward Andrew Finnegan.

"Do you think he has helped you make good decisions?"

"Yes, a bunch of times, especially in trusting my own judgment. Drew also reminds me what I've done to help my mom. He was right about my birth mom, too. She didn't show up at camp as she said she would. Two times we made a date, and she never came."

"I'm sorry, Phoebe. That must have hurt."

"She didn't care when Dad took me away from her, and she doesn't care now. I wish I'd never seen the letter she left. I wouldn't even know about her."

Dr. Landt said, "I think I know you better than that. I imagine you still hope to speak with her, don't you?"

"I hate that she can string me along. It's not a nice feeling at all."

"It's important to put this in your journal because the next time she calls, which I imagine she will, you can recall your reactions to her ambivalence. Phoebe, if you're comfortable talking about it, how is your mom doing?"

"I think OK. Dr. Gordon has been updating Dad on possible release times. She has to remain on her medication at home, though. I worry the stress of Dad and Barbara could cause a relapse."

"You have about a week till school starts. Your mom will probably be home soon. Will she be going back to work?"

"She wants to, Dr. Landt, but she's saying that Barbara spread rumors about her. If it's true, I don't know how to prove it. Dad tried to talk to me at camp last week, but how can I accept the two of them together? I'd feel completely disloyal to

Mom. I wish I could make him understand how Barbara isn't the wonderful person he thinks she is."

"If you feel this strongly, ask your father to come to a session here with you."

I was determined to persuade Dad to agree to come with me the next time as Drew drove us back to the Sinks'.

I asked him, "Do you think you could convince Dad to stay at the house with me until Mom gets home? Maybe Barbara or Jackie will slip up while he's here. Then he'd see for himself what they're really like."

"Sure, I'll try to talk to him." Drew said.

During the remainder of the week, Sharon and I finished reading our assigned summer books and shopped for school supplies.

Dad came back on Saturday to stay for the first week of school. He smiled, but that smile did not reflect in his eyes. We went to the house and had a quiet lunch together. I set the table while he unwrapped the sandwiches he'd bought at the deli.

"When I saw how you felt finding the birth certificate, I could only blame myself. If you want to find Keira, you should. But you have too much going on now, and this may not be the right time, but if you want my help, I'm here for you."

My stomach did a forward roll because I wasn't ready to tell him that I had already talked with her. "Can you come to Dr. Landt with me on Wednesday?"

"I promise I'll go with you. No excuses this time."

After school on Monday, I vacuumed and had dinner ready when Dad drove in. As he looked over my math homework, I tried to imagine his moving back here and had to ask Dad what he was planning.

"When Mom leaves the hospital, where are you going to be?"

He stopped working and looked up. "You know I can't stay here, honey. I've taken an apartment in New York."

"But you're going to be in Maple Ridge. To see Barbara."

"I have to work out a schedule, yes."

"How are you going to have time to check on Mom?"

He stood up to give me a hug.

"I'll still be conferencing with Dr. Gordon, Phoebe. He calls me with updates. But you have been fantastic. You are her rock, not me. I'm the disappointment. I left because I was making her worse. She'll get her job back and go on from there. I'm very sad this is the end to what was a great beginning."

I answered, "I've had weeks to go over this. And what's really sad is your blind trust of Barbara."

The following Wednesday afternoon, he picked me up from school for our appointment with Dr. Landt who focused on Dad first as he sat next to me on the couch. "Do you have a main concern about your separation with Patrice?"

Dad explained, "I've lost trust from my daughter. I don't want her to think that I'm giving up on her. That's already an issue with lying to her about her birth mother. I need to give her support now, not distance."

"You obviously love and care for your daughter, but how do you think you can help Phoebe?"

Dad said, "I'm hoping you can give some guidance."

Dr. Landt said, "I'd like to hear from Phoebe."

I didn't want to start complaining, but it came out like a whine. All the crap I was telling him about Jackie wasn't sinking in. "I hate that Dad's siding with Jackie. He won't believe what's going on with her."

Dad responded half to me and half to Dr. Landt, "There has to be a middle road between what the two girls are saying. I believe that Phoebe is feeling left out and that Jackie might take her place. That couldn't be further from what I want."

I reminded him, "Barbara always comes first, and you believe everything she says."

"Phoebe, I'm doing my best. I know you don't like Barbara and me together, but she's been incredibly supportive. I feel happy for the first time in years."

221

And there was the awful truth. I had to speak up. "She's a bloodsucker. She moved in on her best friend's husband. You can't get any lower than that."

Dr. Landt said to both of us, "Families split up and you, Phoebe, are trying to make sense out of one of the worst scenarios. Charles, you're in a position now to make the separation easy or difficult. The first step is to communicate, and I think Phoebe is trying to do this. It's up to you, Charles, to listen to her concerns whether or not you think they are valid. Phoebe, is there anything else you feel that's important for your father to hear?"

She was looking at me in an encouraging kind of way, so I just let it out. "I already found Keira Leighton, talked with her, and set up a meeting."

I'd never seen Dad look so surprised. "You found her yourself and met with her already?"

I was shivering with nerves and looked right at him. "I didn't want to wait for someone to make decisions for me. Keira and I talked, but she didn't show up twice to meet me."

He sighed. "I'm so sorry, PS. That's what I was afraid of." He took both my hands in his. "I never wanted you to feel rejected by her. You are everything that Keira was not. She doesn't deserve you."

"I'd still like answers. She says she'll come, but doesn't show up or call."

Dr. Landt said, "Keira could be afraid to meet you. I absolutely do not excuse her treatment of you, but your parents obviously made decisions years ago for your best interest. Let's leave this for now. Your mom should be your priority, and Keira is definitely a serious distraction. So for our next session, the two of you should bring some ideas about how you want to spend time together. Whether it's a regular schedule or just events you can do, that's a start to get through this change in your lives."

As we drove to see Mom in the afternoon, I couldn't find one thing to say in the car until we got to the parking lot.

"Maybe it's best you stay here, Dad. I'll text if she's up to a visit with you."

Mom and I met in the community room again, and I noticed a difference almost immediately. The far-off stare was gone, the interruptions and subject changes were in control. I said, "You look so much better. How did the last visit go with Dr. Gordon?'

"He said the same. And I don't feel as hyper. It's such a relief not to be running a marathon, trying to take care of everyone. I know I wasn't the best mother for the last few months."

"Let's talk about what's up ahead. I made this for you, Mom," as I handed her a card.

She opened the envelope and read, "I've missed you more than you know. I'm so happy we'll be together again soon." On it, I sketched two riders jumping over a stone wall.

Mom said, "This is so beautiful. I know exactly why you drew this, and you've got me thinking about going riding. It was such a huge part of growing up, and now I'll be able to enjoy it with you."

"Has it been really awful here, Mom?"

She sighed. "I knew I couldn't go on like I did, and this was the only option. At least your father found the best doctors. I'll hand him that. But these last few weeks have been the longest I've ever experienced. When I'm here, this is the new normal and I'm talking with people who have similar problems."

"Does it help talking with other patients?"

"You remember Gina? Her husband died and she fell apart. Sharing what's going on makes me realize how insignificant my own problem is compared to someone else's. So sometimes, I could end up helping a friend."

It occurred to me how this visit wasn't accompanied by my usual anxiety and stomach cramps. I was listening to Mom's reasoned sentences and being able to focus on what comes next. All good omens. I could see her old self again.

Dad was already sitting in Dr. Gordon's office being advised on Mom's release. As I took my seat, he said, "Patrice has improved enough that we expect her to leave the hospital before the weekend. I recommend that she continue with counseling as an outpatient once she's home. We can set up the initial appointments today."

On the Friday of Labor Day weekend, Mom walked through our front door with Drew and me. Her eyes swept the neatly organized living room with a regretful remembrance of a particular day more than eight weeks ago. Mom's previous purchases were either stored or donated, eliminating the chaos and clutter. I'd hoped to erase the visual reminder of that living nightmare. "It'll be different now, Phoebe. I promise," as she carried her suitcase upstairs to her bedroom.

Drew and I took groceries to the kitchen to make lunch for us to have on the patio. My phone buzzed as Mom gathered plates and napkins for the table. "Hi, Dad."

"Just checking in. Glad that Drew was available. Everything OK?"

"Are you in Maple Ridge, Dad?"

"No, Connecticut if you need me. I'm visiting a colleague."

"Did you want to come by here?" I asked.

"Let's let your mom get used to being by herself at the house first. Then we'll talk about it."

After lunch, I served a welcome-home cake that was her favorite (chocolate raspberry). "Delicious and sorely missed," she said.

Drew lounged and was fine with relaxing here for the weekend. Mom read until she got restless and went for a walk. "To be able to just go out and not have to be monitored…how nice," she commented.

After an early dinner Mom said, "You have no idea how often I looked forward to sleeping in my own bed," as she stood on the landing. "See you in the morning, and please don't wake me."

"Good night, Mom. Hope you sleep well." I called upstairs.

I looked to Drew. "Thanks for staying. I was hopeful the homecoming would be this easy, but wasn't really sure what to expect."

He commented, "Living in Greenwich with my mom offered a bit of practice with verbal explosions. Glad you didn't need backup. I'll wait till Monday to leave for the city. Maybe Patrice'd like a couple of her friends to stop by."

She wanted to rest most of Saturday, but I was encouraged at her willingness to go on a couple of long walks together.

When Sharon stopped by with some flowers on Monday, Mom told her, "Finding a good friend is hard, and Phoebe is so lucky to have you. Thanks for taking care of her."

"There were perks involved. Phoebe promised me a car. That's the only reason I put up with her," she joked.

The phone rang after school on Tuesday with the police asking for Mrs. Spring. Officer Lundy said it would be best if she came in to the station on her own. Shocked and unsure how to answer, I frantically blurted out, "She's not available," as my heart pounded and my stomach flipped. I didn't lie, because she was asleep. "I'll have her call you as soon as possible."

I phoned Dad immediately. The Board of Trustees President of Family Assistance had just called him about an audit that had uncovered missing funds, and Mom was suspected.

Dad told me, "I'm coming back to town. Wait until I call our attorney, Alan, before having Mom contact the police. He'll go with your mother to the station, but you should stay home."

"I can't Dad, I'm going with her. Mom needs me now. She has no one else."

Within the hour, Alan, Mom and I found Dad waiting for us at the Maple Ridge police station. Mom was very upset and defensive when we first met with Officer Lundy. I asked to be present during their meeting because I could see that she was visibly shaken.

Mom became frustrated when the officers insisted several times that she must have had some knowledge of a $9,000 deposit to her bank account.

She stated, "This was a complete surprise. I was in the hospital for the last eight weeks. I had no knowledge of this."

Officer Lundy said, "Can you tell us about your history at Family Assistance?"

Mom replied, "I started as a volunteer when I was in college and worked my way up to the accounting responsibilities that I do, or did, up till now."

Officer Lundy said, "What about other employees or volunteers at the office? Does anyone have access to the company accounts?"

She answered, "I have the passwords, along with the officers of the agency. We have a fundraising committee, but I don't believe they can access the money or the accounts."

After hearing such serious questions, I remembered dismissing Mom's insistence about how Barbara had submarined her job, but now it seemed believable. We left the building, and Mom's hands were shaking. I called Dr. Gordon but the call went to voicemail while she was confronting my dad.

"I know you don't want to hear it, Charles, but I swear that Barbara Lorrenze has something to do with this. I already told Phoebe that your love interest has been on a rampage at work to discredit me. One person warned me just before I cracked up and ended in the hospital."

Alan shut down the shout-fest by suggesting that Charles leave while we went over to the bank. We waited in the manager's office for the paperwork to come back to view the account information. The $9,000 was transferred to Mom's savings account on the afternoon that she was taken to the hospital. She couldn't have made the transaction.

Alan called Officer Lundy to clear Mom from any connection to the embezzlement of funds. Now it was up to the police to figure out who did it.

Dr. Gordon returned my call, and after I explained the day's stressful events, he recommended letting Mom rest. He didn't want to change or add another medication unless it was necessary.

When Alan dropped us off, Mom looked exhausted. She went to bed right away but said as I left her room, "Is this nightmare over yet?"

I shrugged my shoulders and said, "One down and a few more to go it would seem. Have a nap and we'll eat dinner together later."

I started homework. Damn, I missed Sharon for math help and Mom was too stressed to help. I heated up some butternut squash soup that she liked and woke her up. She wasn't hungry, but we sat down together while I finished off a bowl plus half a turkey sandwich. Mom ate a piece of toast with a few slurps and put her spoon down. She lined up her pills and said, "I may as well go over the medication list with you now, Phoebe. Dr. Gordon insisted. I have an appointment on Thursday with him."

"I'm glad your home, Mom. We'll get through this."

She smiled, wished me pleasant dreams, and went upstairs.

The next morning, Mom was still asleep when I left to catch the school bus. I made a short list of a few things that she could pick up at the store hoping she'd go out on her own. Sharon and I walked to most of our classes together until lunchtime. I took my phone from the locker and saw a message from Dad to call him.

"Hi, what's up?"

"I was hoping I'd talk to you before you got home. How are you doing? If there's any worry, I want to know."

"Alan told you that she was completely cleared by the bank of taking funds, right? She was so tense from all the questions yesterday that she really didn't want to eat, but I made her soup."

"Drew offered to stop in. He'll be there this afternoon for anything you might need."

"OK. Gotta go, Dad."

At the end of the day, Sharon and I made a date for Saturday to go riding.

I called as I walked in the front door, "Hey, Mom, I'm back."

Drew answered, "Come in the living room. I've got news."

I gave him a hug following his announcement of starting his new job soon. It was for the medical technician position he wanted.

Mom said, "I asked Drew if he'd take me to the grocery store. I'm embarrassed to go by myself. Sorry to make a fuss."

We took Drew's car to the supermarket for Mom's first trip out. In the second aisle, a couple of her friends stopped us to say how great it was that she was home. "You look really good, Patrice. Call if you need anything." Paula Brice was from Family Assistance and had sent Mom a couple of get-well cards.

Mom thanked her and said after she left, "She's the one who told me about Barbara's being so hateful behind my back just before my episode," which she quoted with her fingers.

We picked up the things on the list and were at the checkout when Barbara and Jackie walked into the store. I thought Mom was going to faint and I braced for another horrible scene. Barbara ignored us, but of course, Jackie mouthed, "You suck," at me. I looked over at Drew's angry expression, and I bumped him shaking my head. Not now.

I thought Mom was doing better than expected, but as we left the store she was in tears. "It's too soon. I can't handle living in the same town as that woman."

Drew said, "Patrice, I guarantee she'll lose any friend she has when the truth is exposed. You and Phoebe will be fine."

We decided to make a reservation for an early dinner in Pleasantville to congratulate Drew on his job. It was time we celebrated some good news. After our meal, Mom suggested to him, "Why don't you have your friends come here for the weekend?"

"That would be great. I'll give Sam and James a call later. I have to go to the city tomorrow, but we can be here Friday evening."

Drew was staying the night thankfully, because he was working with me on my math homework. Obviously he was trying to help out. I wondered how Drew's mom, Darleen, would look at the situation. It hurt my head to think about it too much.

Ellen Sinks and Mom's friend, Gloria, stopped by with fruit and a gift basket. Gloria asked Mom to join her at the candidates' debate for the up-coming election, leaving her to think about possibly volunteering again.

"Would that be something you'd enjoy, Mom?" I asked after they left.

"I've always been interested in national politics, but not so much the local elections. Let's find out if I have a paid job first. Then I'll think about being involved with a volunteer group. I'm going to bed. It's been a long day, and Phoebe, thank you for being the best daughter I could ever want."

Mom's unintentional double-edged compliment meant I couldn't bring up my birth certificate now.

Friday at our lockers, I told Sharon I had a surprise and asked her to come for dinner. I took the bus home and Sharon called me. "Did you see the paper today?" I skipped to the kitchen to find it. "Holy cow, it's on the front page."

"After an unnamed employee was questioned in relation to missing funds from a Maple Ridge organization that offers transitional shelter and services to families, charges were filed for theft of public money and falsifying records according to the district attorney's office. A recent audit discovered the misappropriation of funds."

"Wow, Sharon. I need more info before I show this to Mom. Maybe her friend Paula from work will know something about it. Don't forget, dinner's in an hour."

I found Mrs. Brice's number and phoned her while Mom was upstairs. I explained why I was calling.

She said, "I've only heard some of what happened. Barbara was our main fundraiser. She was somehow able to divert federal grant money that the agency received into a bank account that didn't belong to her. She was questioned and is on unpaid leave until it's settled. Nobody understands why she would do that."

I understood completely, and thanked her for the update.

Mrs. Brice questioned, "Do you think Patrice is coming back to us? I've missed her."

"She's doing well, so thank you. I'll let her know you asked," I said.

As soon as I hung up my phone buzzed. "Oh hi, Dad. Are you calling to apologize?"

"What did I do this time?"

"If you haven't heard, it's in the newspaper today. Go ask Barbara about her interview."

"Phoebe, just tell me what it is. I don't care for the sarcasm."

"It was a headline today. Barbara was questioned for stealing money from Family Assistance. Someone she works with told me."

Silence. "That may not be true."

"That's the problem. You don't listen to me or to Mom. Please let me know when you take our word."

"I'm listening to you now Phoebe, and I want to help. Have you spoken to Keira again?"

I answered, "When she didn't show up twice for meeting a daughter she abandoned, her un-said message was clear enough."

"I'll come by right now if you want me to. Would that help?"

"It's all right. Drew's coming with his friends in a little while. No more drama for now. I'm not bringing Keira up yet to Mom, either. She was pretty stressed this week."

Sharon arrived, and was excited to see Drew, Sam, and James who were staying for the weekend. We let the guys do the grilling while we cut up the vegetables and salad.

Mom noticed how Sharon and I were shamefully flirting. "What are you two up to? It's pretty obvious you know Drew's friends from somewhere. What's going on here?"

"Oh, we saw them at Drew's place in the city. No big deal," I answered quickly. Mom gave me that "I know you're fibbing look", and waited for the real story.

Sharon piped up and said, "We went to the city one Sunday, and we met Drew and the guys downtown. That's all."

Mom looked sharply at Drew. "Whatever they said," he grunted with a smirk.

Mom did great during dinner. No more manic disconnected sentences. She was really on the way back to being Mom. Drew helped Sharon and me clean up, and we sat around the living room listening to college dorm stories.

"I'm going to bed now. It's nice to have company again. Goodnight everyone," Mom said. Sharon and I turned in later, leaving the guys talking downstairs.

Saturday morning was a hoot with Sam and James making eggs and sausages for everyone. Mom cheerfully helped with cleanup before driving us to the stable.

The Saturday riding lesson went so well that Doris was amazed at the progress I made over the summer. We practiced a course of eight fences with a change of direction when Doris commented, "You're so much more confident now, Phoebe. I can see the difference in how you're communicating with Postman. He's responding so well to everything you're asking of him."

"My trainer at camp told me exactly what you said back in June. It just sunk in finally," I admitted.

When we led the horses into the barn, I told Sharon, "I need to tell Mom that I talked to Keira. Dad was cool about it, but I wonder what Mom's reaction will be."

Sharon said, "I'd think she'd be more upset if you don't tell her soon. Think of your reaction about learning the big secret. She's probably more worried about how to tell you the truth."

"I have to speak up now, but I'm not looking forward to it," I replied.

Drew, Sam and James were joking around Saturday evening. When he saw me pull out the birth certificate, he nodded.

He called his crew together and went for a drive as Mom came into the living room. "I need to show you something, Mom."

We sat on the couch together as I said, "I know what happened, Mom. I found this last month."

She saw the certificate and was crushed. She turned white and sobbed as she put her hands up to her face. "I don't know why I was so afraid. I thought that once you found her she'd tell you some pathetic story and convince you to leave. Your father was always against withholding the truth."

"Dad told me how he got custody. I wish you'd have listened to him and just told me. I wish I hadn't found out like I did because I felt like you didn't trust me to know what really happened. I want to meet Keira, but don't fall apart, Mom. I'm not going anywhere."

I reached for her hand, but she got up and walked across the room. "Before your fifteenth birthday, I was going to tell you. I planned it. Then everything happened at once. The complaints at work, your father, Barbara, the breakdown."

I said, "I also found the letter she wrote to you."

"She was keeping track of where we live. Charles wasn't paying her alimony once she re-married, but when her letter came in the mail, I panicked. I knew I wasn't thinking clearly, so I took more medication, and I fell apart. Her letter last year made it clear she wouldn't leave us alone. Then Charles and I were having so many problems, and I still couldn't tell you."

"Mom, please don't worry 'cause I'm not going anywhere, but if Keira wants to see me, I won't refuse."

I could tell Mom didn't expect that, but I wasn't going to lie. I heard Drew and the guys come back in the house, and I looked over to her. "You OK, Mom?"

She nodded but went upstairs.

Early Sunday morning my phone buzzed interrupting the awkward silence between Mom and me having breakfast together. Andrew was calling. I quickly stepped outside to talk to him for over half an hour.

"Hey, Peebes, how's the school year going?"

"More drama both bad and good – beginning with the crazy girl, mom at home, my best friend, and a brother who's become a temporary housemate."

Andrew said, "No wonder I didn't hear from you. I've been busy too with track meets all over the place. When can we get together? I've been hoping you'd call to let me know."

"When's your first day off from classes? We could go for a ride then."

He said, "Let's make it for Saturday. I won't have to go home so early."

I gave him directions to the house, and we signed off as I wandered into the kitchen to see Drew and the guys eating breakfast.

I announced to Drew, "Well, the good news is Andrew's coming Saturday to go riding and meet Mom, and Mom and I finally talked about Keira last night."

"Good. That's progress. How 'bout telling Dad what you're doing this time, and be prepared if the woman doesn't appear again," he said, taking the orange juice from the fridge. "I think he'd like to be a part of this, you know. He said something to me the other day."

"What?" I asked.

"He wasn't around when you needed him this year. It's weighing on him. He'd like to be in your life more."

"I've been talking about Dad with Dr. Landt, so maybe he could come to another appointment with me. I blew up last time. I told him I don't want some teary reunion with Keira. I just want to see her. I've always wondered why I didn't look like anyone in this family."

We heard a car coming up the driveway. I looked out the window to see a red Chevy making tracks all over our lawn. It was Jackie. Drew bolted out the door while pulling out his phone. Mom was right behind me as Drew yelled outside, "Get out of here before I call the police!" He videoed her driving circles around and through the garden alongside the house. Jackie got stuck and backed out leaving two huge gouges near the turn-around. She left more tire tracks by the driveway as we watched her exit.

"This has got to end, Phoebe," Drew said as the guys checked out the damage and snapped photos.

The stomach churning idea of making a complaint against her would be talked about for months at school. Everyone would know about Dad and Mrs. Lorrenze, Mom in lock up, and all the crap fueling our feud. I guess Jackie didn't care about the gossip.

Drew picked up the phone and called Mrs. Lorrenze. I was waving my arms and saying, "Nooo!"

He turned his back to me. "This is Drew Spring." He put the call on speaker. "I have a video of your daughter Jackie, who just did a drive-through garden tour on the Spring's lawn in her red Chevy."

Mrs. Lorrenze retorted, "That can't be true. Jackie is right here."

Drew answered, "Mrs. Lorrenze, I'm not calling to argue with you. You need to tell Jackie to keep her distance from Phoebe and Mrs. Spring. No more phone calls, which we have on digital, no more confrontations in public places for which we have witnesses, and no more vandalism, including painting the side of the Spring's house, and destroying their personal property."

Mrs. Lorrenze insisted, "I don't know what you're talking about. You're lying. I'm sure Phoebe did all that herself."

I rolled my eyes as Drew continued, "I assure you, we have proof that Jackie's behavior has escalated from phone calls to stalking. We will not tolerate it. An estimate for repairing the damage to the lawn will be sent to you via Mrs. Spring's attorney. This first complaint will be registered at the high school. They are to be in no classes together and will avoid each other in the hallway. If Jackie continues with one more action of bullying, stalking, threatening, or damage to personal property, we will then contact the police."

She hung up.

"She sounded pissed," I said.

"Notifying the school is the first the step. The next is to go shopping for a security system."

"I need to stay with Mom in case Jackie comes back. I was going to call Sharon and ask her to come over."

"Then I'll go with the guys to the store, so we can install it for you this afternoon."

Finally. Is this going to be the end of Jackie's torment?

Sharon and I got Mom to sit with us outside to enjoy the sunshine while Drew, Sam, and James worked on the outdoor

243

and indoor security system. It was connected to our phones, so we could monitor it even while we weren't there. Mrs. Sinks came over for an early barbecue dinner, helping Sharon and me with the cleanup so Mom could relax.

Our moms talked after dinner. "Phoebe told me that you've been doing OK. Has the transition been difficult?"

Mom sighed, "I had no idea of the complications I left behind for my child." She started to cry. "I'm just finding out about the aftermath of what's been going on with Jackie. I have to end it somehow."

Mrs. Sinks said taking her hand, "I'll accompany you when you go to the school administration because I personally saw one of Jackie's outbursts recently. Phoebe handled it very well, Patrice. She's a lot like you."

Our company said their goodbyes after dinner, leaving the house to just the two of us. I helped her in the kitchen while we chatted about non-threatening subjects.

After school on Monday, on the way to my shrink appointment, Mom told me she and Mrs. Sinks met with Dr. Janus, the principal. The fact that someone else confirmed Jackie's stalking, convinced him to switch Jackie's schedule so that we were no longer in PE class together.

I said, "I've tried to avoid her when this all started. Now maybe she'll have to back off."

"But you must tell Dr. Janus if there is any contact, either physical or cyber from her," Mom insisted.

When I sat down in Dr. Landt's office, I said, "Keira still hasn't called me after the last missed meeting date."

"What emotions are you feeling now? If it's anger, you may have a problem trying to get the answers you're seeking."

"It's not so much anger as wondering if I'm at all like her. If I could meet her, maybe I'd see faults that I have."

Dr. Landt said, "I'd be curious to know if she feels she has control of her gambling habit. That could be why she's not followed through with a face to face meeting."

"Yes, Dad told me how difficult having an addiction is. I don't want to get sucked into another drama situation."

Dr. Landt warned, "If you do contact her again, be up front and ask questions. She'll want to know about you, but try to elicit information about her life."

Mom picked me up and was curious about my sessions. "I'm doing much better since I've seen her, Mom. She helps me find my own way to working on a problem instead of telling me what I should do."

Mom gave my hand a squeeze. "You were already capable of doing that. I'm glad you understand how independent you can be."

We'd been home for five minutes when Paula Brice from Family Assistance called to speak with Mom. "I just wanted to let you know that we found out Barbara was fired today. She used your accounting password to steal the agency grant money, and she stole your bank account information from the employee file. From what I heard, the agency doesn't want the bad press and is negotiating with her on the return of the money in exchange for not being prosecuted, but she's also facing other charges of fraud."

Mom said, "I had no idea she hated me so much. She just wanted me out of the way. Permanently, I guess."

Mrs. Brice replied, "We miss you here at work, Patrice, and I hope you'll be able to come back."

Right after she hung up, another call came in from Family Assistance. President Gerard was asking her to come in to talk with him. Mom hung up and said, "Well, this week, I'll know if I have a job or not."

"Be positive, I bet he'll offer you..."

The sound of crunching gravel in our driveway cut me off. When all the outside security lights popped on, the red car quickly turned around to scoot out. It was Jackie. The timing obviously involved Mom's earlier meeting with Principal Janus and the news of her mother's firing from work. I said, "Now that we have the video cameras hooked up, we have proof she's stalking. Maybe she'll finally get the hint."

Mom went upstairs just before my phone buzzed. I almost didn't accept the call because it was Keira once again.

I answered, "Keira, why are you calling when you obviously don't want contact?"

Keira said, "I'm... very nervous to meet you. It's not embarrassment. One thing about me, Phoebe, is that I don't like to be judged, and I can tell you're already judging. So, I was thinking it would be better to meet over coffee or a soda. Your camp was too far."

Remembering what Dr. Landt said about wanting answers, I asked, "How old are Brittney and Kevin, Keira?" I tried to control the edge in my voice.

"I'd really like to see you before we talk more in depth about our lives," she pressed.

"Just a simple answer please, Keira." I wasn't letting this go.

"She'll be twelve, and he's ten," she admitted.

"And they live with you?" But I already guessed the answer.

"Yes. Here in Stamford."

She had only stopped gambling five years ago, but she has been able to somehow care for my half-siblings. I was done with the conversation.

"I've heard enough. Goodbye, Keira," and hung up.

Mom came in. I stood up and went over to her, crying. She saw the phone in my hand and heard who was on the other end of the line.

"That was Keira, wasn't it? What happened?"

"I didn't ask her any of the real questions I wanted to know. I just hung up."

"You'll find the words you need when you're ready," she said. I wished I'd not even taken the call.

I showed Mom my journal, and we went through every question that I had for Keira. How can a mother give up her child? Did Keira care that Mom took me away? She kept the second born daughter, why not me? Why did she take so long to write to Mom?

What became clear to me was how much Mom cared which seemed the opposite of my self-centered birth mother.

CHAPTER 19   APOLOGIES

I called Dad later to see if we could meet on Saturday. I lobbed Jackie's latest trip to our driveway at him. "The security system Drew and the guys installed is working great. All the house lights came on, and she took off. So I think we're good for now. And Andrew is coming for a visit over the weekend if you want to meet him. He's driving here Saturday to go riding with me."

"You must like him. Would you want to have lunch?"

"Can we go after riding? We'll be through around twelve thirty. Or maybe we could go into the city to see you," I suggested.

Dad said, "Let's say I'll pick you up at the house when you two are done."

I guided Andrew into our kitchen Saturday morning to meet Mom.

He held out his hand to Mom. "I'm Andrew, Mrs. Spring. Thanks for inviting me here."

She offered coffee and poured two mugs for us.

"I heard about your mother's riding accident. Have you been able to visit her in Massachusetts?" Mom asked.

"Yes, last weekend. She has two more weeks to go in her cast. It's driving her crazy, but she's getting around. She can't wait to ride Tango again. She asked when Phoebe would be coming back to visit, Mrs. Spring."

Mom said to me, "I suppose that would be possible for a day trip once Andrew's mother is back on both feet." My eyebrows about hit the ceiling when I heard that.

We took Andrew's car to the barn as I caught him up on the latest events. On the last leg of our two-hour trail tour on Waterboy and Quincy, we crossed the main road and passed a few groundskeepers trimming trees near Stone Barns.

I brought up Keira as we walked along the bridal path. "My birth mother called again. I pretty much hung up on her I was so angry. She had two kids after me, and they're a wonderful happy family, I'm sure."

"Didn't you tell me she was from Stamford?" he asked.

"Yes. I looked up her address. She's near the water."

Andrew said, "Why don't you come to my house next weekend, and we'll check out where she lives. It's close to Greenwich."

I protested, "Isn't that kind of what Jackie was doing to me? Coming to my home, trying to disrupt my life? So, would that make me a stalker too…if I spied on Keira?"

Andrew mimicked binoculars with his hands, "I suppose you'd have to take it to an extreme level to call it that."

I didn't notice the yellow jackets around us, but they found Waterboy, stinging him several times. Startled, but with legs gripped tightly, I maneuvered Waterboy through the first two bucks but lost my seat on the third. In frighteningly slow motion, I was propelled into a javelin-like fallen branch. Screaming in pain, I looked down and was sickened by the sight of blood spilling on the trail from a deep gash in my upper thigh. Seconds later, Andrew was at my side speaking calmly, and applying pressure to the wound.

The tree workers heard me yelling and came running over to us, calling 911 with our location the moment they saw what happened. One guy stayed to help, but the sight of my leg caused the second guy to be sick. The third guy ran back to the main road to flag the ambulance.

I was in so much pain and getting light-headed as I said, "Andrew, here, get my phone and call Mom and Dad to ask them to go to the hospital."

The emergency crew was quick, but I was really scared on the way to the hospital, even though the EMT's kept assuring me I'd be fine. They wheeled me into a room at the ER, and shortly after I spotted Mom and Dad talking to the doctor. "I assume you're Phoebe's parents?"

Dad said, "Yes, how is she?"

"She has lost a lot of blood. We've started a transfusion, but her blood type is very rare. We can get it, but if either of you is B negative, it helps to keep the supply available."

Dad looked at Mom. She knew exactly what he was thinking. He said, "I believe her birth mother is B negative. I'll call her."

Mom was sitting next to the bed looking stressed when Andrew poked his head in. "Is it all right if I say hi?" he asked.

I guess my face lit up, because Mom waved him inside while she stepped out.

"You're definitely looking better, but your mom, not so much."

I glanced around the room and couldn't help crying. "I'm really worried about her. She didn't need this to happen now. What if it's too much for her to handle?"

Andrew handed me a tissue. "If the ER doctor can reassure her, she'll know you're OK."

"I didn't tell you...I think she's going to be offered her job back. The head of the agency called to meet with her next week. I can't believe I might ruin this for her."

"You didn't ruin anything. It was a freak accident. Your mom knows that. It's not going to stop her from going back to work anymore than it'll stop you from riding again."

We could hear Mom outside the door. "I almost lost her, Charles. She could have died out there," she said.

"Phoebe always rides with someone and Andrew knew exactly what to do. So it wasn't a tragedy. Patrice, please try to see that Phoebe is safe and monitored. Don't make this accident into a case of what-ifs."

Mom said, "I know, I know. I can't help it. What happened to your ex-wife? I thought she was coming."

"As you're aware, she was never the most dependable of people," Dad answered.

After staying at the hospital for over two hours, they both knew Keira wouldn't be coming. Mom came in later to tell me we could go home. I rode with Mom while Dad and Andrew followed in their cars. Mom said, "You were right about Andrew. He's considerate and responsible, and I like him."

I replied, "I can talk to him about anything, Mom. He's so different from other boys I've met. He asked me to go to Greenwich next weekend."

As we turned into the driveway Mom said, "Let's see how you're feeling next week. Then we'll look at the calendar to see what day would be best."

Andrew opened my car door and helped me walk up the front steps. I liked how he started the conversation as soon as we walked in the house.

He explained, "After you left in the ambulance, I took both horses back to the stable, so that took some time, 'cause we were pretty far out. Everyone wanted to know what happened to you. I already called Doris, but you should let her know you're OK, too. Waterboy had quite a few stings."

I said, "And he sure let me know about it."

"You really scared me, there, Peebes. Please don't do that again," he tugged on my hair.

Dad said, "I think you should be looking at medicine instead of engineering, Andrew. The way you handled the whole situation is very commendable."

Andrew looked around, embarrassed probably.

Mom came in with iced tea. "Phoebe, you need to eat. I put some steaks on the grill for everyone, and they should be ready soon."

Dad got up, thanked Andrew again, and headed for the door. "I should get back to New York."

"I haven't seen you all week, though. We missed our lunch date, so can't you at least stay for an early dinner, Dad?"

I was giving him the doggie eyes, and he gave up. "All right."

"Phoebe, can we talk in the kitchen?" he asked.

I limped after him for a refill. I sighed saying, "I heard the nurse ask you and Mom about another donor. She didn't show, did she?"

"When I spoke to Keira she was surprised, but she agreed to come. I don't excuse what she did back then or today, but if you shut her out completely, you'll never learn anything about her."

"Dad, I think when you say something and don't follow through, you aren't being honest. She lost her chance."

"I understand, but later on, you may want answers. I'll contact her for you and make sure she's sincere the next time."

"Go ahead if you want, but I doubt I'll change my mind."

After dinner, Dad said goodbye, and I had a chance to talk with Andrew. "Dad likes you. He told me. And Mom, too," I said.

"Well, I like you. And we'll go on the trails again soon, right?"

Mom went upstairs giving us some privacy. We were in a lip-lock when she walked back into the room with a loud attention-getting cough.

Mom said, "It's getting late, Andrew. You should be on your way home now but do come back soon. Thank you so much for your quick thinking."

I joked, "Long day, wasn't it?" hobbling with him to the door.

He said, "Can't wait for the next one," with a really nice kiss.

The next morning, Mom seemed nervous about her upcoming meeting at Family Assistance. "I need to pick an outfit for my appointment with Bill Gerard. I'm not sure what fits me now."

Sharon came over and we critiqued all of her suits, deciding on a blue one. She wasn't sure until Sharon commented, "Wow, Mrs. Spring, you look terrific." I agreed.

Sharon followed me into the kitchen for a snack. "You know, Phoebe, I'm reminding you that Andrew can't take my place riding. You're going to have to double-book when he comes here again."

"Either that or clone myself. He was so great after the accident. He didn't even get sick at the mess I left behind. How cool is that?"

"How's your leg today?" Sharon asked.

"Still sore, but it could have been so much worse."

She said, "I can help with your books tomorrow between classes."

I said, "Climbing steps is the problem. Maybe I can use the elevator for a day or two until the stitches heal. Mom's going to drive me in the morning."

When Sharon left, I asked Mom, "Do you want your job back, really, or are you just saying that because everyone's expecting you to go to work right away?"

She said, "I'm a bit worried about the meeting this week. Sometimes my medication makes me a little foggy. I have an appointment with Dr. Gordon at the hospital on Tuesday, and I'll mention it then."

"But, do you feel ready to go back to work? I'd hate to see you overwhelmed again, especially with all that's happened in the last couple of weeks."

"I've known Bill for years. He won't have me if there's any doubt on his part about my abilities. So we'll see."

I spent the rest of the day on my homework and helped Mom prepare dinner. We were almost normal.

Sharon and I were having lunch on Tuesday, when one of the teachers said I was needed in the principal's office. I asked Sharon to come because I was expecting the worst. Dr. Janus asked me to sit down and said, "There's been an accident, and your mom is at Phelps hospital. She is OK, but Mr. Spring called to say he's coming to pick you up in a few minutes."

I got the dizzy head again and asked for some water. "What happened to her?"

"I'm told that she was walking and was struck by a car, but she is doing all right. You'll wait here in my office for your father."

We were at the hospital within the hour and found Mom sitting up in bed with no broken bones, but with bruises along her left side and right leg. She had already gone through X-rays and MRI.

"We need a frequent family plan here, Mom. What happened to you?"

"I was in the crosswalk after my meeting with Bill Gerard when someone didn't stop. It was Barbara Lorrenze," she said pointedly.

My face dropped. How is this woman still running loose?

Mom said, "She was furious that I was getting my job back. Barbara was yelling at me when I was sprawled on the pavement."

Dad went white.

Drew was waiting at home for us with takeout from Pizza Palace when Mom was released from the hospital. He pulled two beers from the fridge giving one to Dad as I set the table.

Dad said as he sat down, "Patrice, I'm really sorry you were hurt. I didn't listen to you."

She answered, "I didn't want to believe it myself. Do we need to worry that Phoebe could be threatened next?"

Dad said, "I don't think so. Barbara's house is up for sale. She won't be living in Maple Ridge much longer. Jackie moved to her father's months ago. He's sending her to a private school starting next week."

Mom asked him, "How do you know all this already?"

"After what happened, I called the police to report Barbara's stalking. I was still getting her emails and texts. I had to block her calls. She's going to need an attorney. At the very least for negligent driving."

There was silence.

Dad spoke up, "Both of you, Phoebe and Patrice, I'm very sorry about refusing to believe you these past months. I ignored what you said. The abuse you suffered from Barbara and Jackie was inexcusable. I know it hasn't shown, but I'm very proud of my kids. You stood up to everything thrown at you, Phoebe, and Drew was there for you every time. I'm very lucky to have you both."

"Is anyone able to share some good news?" I asked.

Drew said, "I'm employed."

"Finally," Dad clapped. "I can stop paying your rent."

Drew added, "And I appreciate that Dad didn't make me live out of my car. The tech lab is only a twenty-minute walk from the apartment."

I said, "I have a local history project coming up. Sharon and I are partnering on a documentary of Rockefeller State Park.

We've already got some state people to interview for our video presentation."

Dad said, "The case I was working on all summer was settled, so back to normal hours."

Mom's eyes took in each of us. "My daughter never stopped believing in me. Who could ask for more than that?"

We were quiet for a moment.

Dad said, "Goodnight, everyone," as he pulled out his car keys. I'll be checking with you later this week, Phoebe." Drew spoke to him briefly at the door then flopped on the couch next to me before grabbing the remote.

I could hear the water running in the kitchen as Mom was loading the dishwasher. I asked Drew, "What did you say to him?"

Drew hesitated, "I asked about Barbara. He said he'll have nothing to do with her after the mess she created."

"That's what he should have said two months ago. Everyone says that men's brains are in their pants. Now I understand."

The phone rang, and I climbed over Drew to answer it.

"Well, Patrice," the caller said. "You won. You got Charles back. Congratulations."

"Mrs. Lorrenze?" I said. "This is Phoebe. Don't bother my mom again," and hung up seeing Drew's surprised expression. "She thought I was Mom, and I thought we were finally done."

Wednesday morning, I was eating breakfast with Mom, when Drew offered to drive me to school on his way to New York. He stacked my books in the car, and moved the passenger seat back before helping me into place. The five-day old leg booboo was healing but still sore.

As we drove through town, we both saw Dad's Mini go by, and he wasn't alone. The passenger seat carried an attractive brunette who didn't look familiar. "Do you know who that was with Dad?" I asked Drew.

"No. He said he was staying with someone from the office yesterday."

"Oh, my God. You don't think he's already got someone else lined up, do you?" I questioned.

"From past experience, he does have a tough time going it alone."

"You'll tell me, right? Mom should find out sooner rather than later. She still loves him, you know."

Drew reminded me, "Just concentrate on that Rockefeller Park project which sounds pretty challenging."

I avoided Jackie the entire day. We had different lunch periods and no more PE together, but a lot of kids heard about Barbara's driving incident, as I could see the strange looks on several faces. Sharon and I took our study period to plan for the park video.

CHAPTER 20   HOME

After school, I came home to find a package sitting on the kitchen counter with Keira's return address. Mom was busy preparing the chicken for later, and I couldn't judge her reaction. I waited a sec, hoping the unexpected arrival hadn't tipped her emotional basket.

"Hey, Mom, you OK?"

"I'll recover. It was just a shock. Every time I hear her name pop into a conversation, is like nails on a chalkboard."

"Weird that Keira sent something considering I hung up on her. Twice."

"That just shows that she wants more."

"Do you want to see what's in the box, Mom?"

Long silence. She replied, "If I don't look now, I'll wonder for the rest of my life."

I got the scissors out and opened it. I lifted out a christening dress, mine, with a note attached.

Now Mom was crying.

"Oh, Mom, please. I'm so sorry. The timing of this couldn't be worse, but at least I told you I found the documents before this came."

She collected herself and sat down hard. "Read the note to me. Get it done," as she wiped her eyes.

"Dear Phoebe,

I've not made a very good first, second, or third impression and hope the little dress will help you understand how much you really mean to me. I have no excuse for not traveling to your camp or for failing to go to the hospital. I simply couldn't gather up the courage to meet with you after leaving you behind so long ago. I thought perhaps your father would be willing to drive you to my home in Stamford. Please call again.

Keira"

Mom's reaction was swift and clear. She grabbed the note and slammed it on the table, startling me enough to jump. "The nerve of that woman. She's setting up a meeting with you, conditional upon seeing your father again."

"Is that what you think? That she just wants to see Dad, not me?"

"Phoebe, have you ever known me to bad mouth someone? Have I ever said cruel or unkind words about anyone? I never met Keira Tierney, but believe me, I know what Keira's capable of doing and the kind of person she is. Charles went through hell to gain full custody of you even with having proof of negligence."

I couldn't explain how, but my mom could determine the sincerity of just about anyone quickly. I knew I should take her anger seriously.

"I'm sorry if it hurts you, Mom, but at some point I should see for myself," as I turned to leave the kitchen.

"The adults in your life have dumped so much undeserved grief and unhappiness on you this summer. The last thing I want is to witness another assault on your heart. Please wait to call her, OK?"

I took the dress upstairs and stuck the ill reminder in a drawer. At dinner, the silence was thick with Mom's and my thoughts colliding. We cleared the plates, and I started upstairs to study. "Phoebe, wait. Let's discuss this. It's best if we leave your father out of it. I think Drew could drive you to see her. He won't be taken in by a phony act."

Mom's giving nature put my problem before her fear. She was closing her eyes to her worst nightmare to help me.

I said, "I think there may be a better idea. I could see Drew getting mad at her, but Andrew knows the whole story. We had talked about doing a ride-by at Keira's house. It's not far from where he lives."

Mom put her arms around me. She was so comforting, I broke down immediately. "PS, I know how strong you are, but you've been holding all these emotions in for too long. Just let it go, Sweetie."

I cried for ten minutes. Just bawled. I couldn't believe I had that much water in me. "I missed you so much, Mom. You have no idea."

"Oh, I think I do."

We decided on Andrew as the better choice. I just had to get through the rest of the week.

I knew Andrew had track practice, so I had to wait till after school Thursday to call him back. "Hey!" He sounded so happy to hear from me.

I said, "Would you be OK with taking me to Keira's house over the weekend?"

"That'd be great. Love to do it. We can stop at my place so you can meet my dad if you want."

"I wish you went to school here, and we could see each other all the time." I said.

"At least the weekends are good. So, I'll come on Saturday?" he asked

"I'll call you later. When I find out for sure from Keira."

We hung up, and I braced myself while punching Keira's number.

The dress arrived yesterday," I said as she picked up.

"I meant what I said in my note. And I'm very sorry for not going to the hospital after your accident," said Keira.

"The doctors were concerned there wouldn't be enough B negative for another emergency. That's why they called you – to keep enough on hand. It's a rare type."

"Are you OK?" she asked.

"Still hurts. Getting around all right, though."

"Sorry again." An uncomfortable silence was broken with, "Do you think your dad might be able to bring you here to Stamford?" she asked.

My stomach was flipping and I was trying to control my shaky voice. "Yes," was all I could get out.

"Would you like to try for Saturday?"

I paused and said, "I think we could make it around one."

"I really am looking forward to seeing you, Phoebe. I'll text the directions to you, OK?"

We hung up. I stood in the kitchen, overthinking what could happen. Would she be mad that Andrew and not Dad arrived with me? Did her kids know yet? Would I blow up in a rage? Was she still married? The list went on. I snapped back to the next call to make. Andrew was fine with picking me up at eleven. We'd have lunch on the way to Stamford, and then go to Keira's house. At least I didn't have to worry about lying to Mom.

Friday crawled along painfully, but Sharon helped a little.

She cautioned, "Remember, she's the one who has to make a good impression. You have nothing to worry about. Just be yourself. Find out what you can while you're with her in case she pisses you off too much, 'cause you might not want to go back there again."

All good points from my best friend.

Mom was pacing around every room in the house Saturday morning.

"Hey, Mom, I'm not ready. Can you get the door, please? Andrew's here." I called downstairs.

I was still taking the stairs slowly, but saw Andrew waiting for me with a huge smile. We shared a quick kiss, not too sloppy, and parked on the couch just glad to be together again.

Mom was hovering, while nervously making a few suggestions.

"Try not to lose it, Sweetie. I know how much talking to Keira means to you."

"I think as long as Andrew's with me, I'll be fine. He's good that way."

"Well, you call if you need anything."

Andrew watched me place my butt on the front seat of his Jeep and pull my legs slowly in. "You're doing pretty good today. You'll be on a horse, I bet, within the month."

"I can't wait. Sharon's so mad I've missed my barn time with her. I have IOUs wracking up for rides together."

The trip to Stamford was quick, only about twenty minutes, so we found a cute place to eat by the water that Andrew knew. With the check paid, and my tummy tightening up, we took a long way to Keira's and sat in the car looking at the neighborhood. Keira's raised ranch style home was on a quiet cul de sac, perfect for kids playing basketball. We were a bit early, so I was feeling antsy. "I think we should just go in now. There's a car in her driveway, so she must be there."

Andrew and I walked up the front steps and knocked, but missed because the door opened abruptly by my birth mother. An awkward silence was broken with her quick greeting.

"Hello, Phoebe."

My stomach had gone from flipping to acid, I guess from lunch, making my hello almost disappear in my throat. It came out like "Uhl" and then a cough and a better "Hello" on the second try.

Then I saw her eyes going back and forth between Andrew and me a number of times. She hesitated for a moment, with the two of us still waiting on the front stoop and muttered, "Um, uh, where's Charles? Is he still in the car?"

I found my voice saying, "My Dad isn't here. This is my friend, Andrew. He offered to drive me today."

"Oh…Oh, I see, so Charles will be coming later, then?"

Wow. Mom was right. My half-baked welcome meant she expected her ex-husband to come with me. She had not opened the door wider or invited us in, so that left me to take control of this uncomfortable meeting. I stood up very straight and said, "Do you want to talk outside, Keira?"

She realized finally that she was being rude and stepped aside to allow us to come in. There was a smell of alcohol as we walked past her, and I shot Andrew a look.

The entryway had stairs going up to the main level and down to a playroom area. We headed up to find the kitchen ahead and the living room to the right, plus a hallway leading left to the bathroom and bedrooms. Andrew and I took a seat on the couch, moving some of the clutter and kids' things aside. Keira offered us coffee. "No, but thank you anyway," we both said.

Keira and I sat looking at each other awkwardly, noticing our similar features. Even though she had aged, much more so than my mom, our roundish faces mirrored the same small mouth, brown eyes, and longer scooped nose, but she had bottle blond hair contrasting with telltale brown eyebrows. No mistake. I was her daughter. She was very slim, almost too much so. I wondered if her ultra thin weight was connected to too much alcohol.

I began, "So, tell me about your job, Keira."

"I'm a nurse, so my hours are pretty long, but I usually get three days a week off. What about you, Phoebe? What are the things you enjoy?"

"Mostly riding and tennis. Weren't you an actress?"

"That didn't last long. I went back to school to finish my degree."

"Where does Mr. Leighton work?" I asked, picking up that Keira was trying not to slur her words.

"My husband's a beverage sales consultant. He travels a lot."

"So, I guess he's not around today."

"Uh, no, actually, we've separated recently, but the kids may be coming home soon."

"Oh, then who cares for the kids when you're working?"

"We share the schedule. He takes them when he can."

"Why'd you want to see me?" I asked.

That was a conversation stopper. She actually looked caught off guard.

"Uh. I thought you wanted to get together, and I kind of owed it to you, I guess."

The door opened, and I froze as I watched a boy and girl walk in. I caught my breath noticing Andrew had the same reaction because the girl was a younger me.

Keira quickly said, "Brittney and Kevin, can you come in with us, please. We have company you should meet."

The girl took three steps and pointed to me. "You're Phoebe, aren't you? Mom told us about you the other day."

"How old are you?" I asked Kevin. He also had his mother's features but in a masculine, boyish way.

"I'm ten. What about you?" he said.

I answered, "I turned fifteen on July 21, and you Brittney?"

"Twelve. Well, I'll be twelve next month...You look like me," which sounded like an accusation.

The kids seemed pleasant enough, but their appearance was disturbing. Both of them were a mess. Their dirty outfits did not come from playing outside. This was real negligence on Keira's part. The greasy hair and ill-fitting clothes didn't make sense. The neighborhood and the house weren't bad, so why didn't Keira notice that her kids looked like they were living on the street? Then it dawned on me that her clothes weren't exactly clean either. So many questions were floating in my head.

I just came out with it. "Why did you want to see my dad, Keira?"

She asked Kevin and Brittney to play downstairs for a while and lifted a glass of water or vodka to her lips. She was crying and her hands were shaking. This was completely unexpected. Andrew handed her some tissues, and we waited till she composed herself.

"I'm having some financial problems," she replied.

I stood bolt upright understanding the reason I was here. She needed money, and Dad was her answer. Furious, I stomped into the kitchen to bring her some water. I could hear Mom's voice in my head, "She's a manipulator. She only cares about herself." No way was I going to get sucked into this situation.

The kitchen had an efficient boxy layout which didn't gel with the stacks of dirty dishes in the sink and on the counter. I looked for ice and found the freezer void of anything but an empty package of hotdogs. Out of curiosity, I opened the fridge door to find no food and a bottle of vodka. There was a half-gallon of milk, no fruit, no vegetables, only some white bread, jelly and condiments on the door, but really nothing for the kids to eat. I called for Andrew.

"Look," as I showed him the bare shelves. "Where's the husband? I wouldn't leave a dog here in this house, let alone two kids."

Half out of anger and the rest disgust, I took my phone and snapped photos of the living conditions including Keira slumped over the side of the couch. Andrew saw me and said, "Get a picture of the kids, too, how they look today. I'll take Kevin outside and shoot some hoops. Maybe I can get the name or number of someone who cares for them. You try Brittney."

As soon as Andrew had Kevin busy, I went downstairs and sat opposite Brittney who was watching cartoons. "Hey." I waited. No response. "How's school, Brittney?"

"OK, I guess."

"When you get home, and if your Mom's working, who comes over to get you dinner? Like your grandmother or grandfather? Or maybe a neighbor?"

"Nobody. Grandma and Grandpa live in Rhode Island. I haven't seen 'em in a while."

"What about your Dad? Do you have his number?"

"Yeah."

"I'd like to tell him I'm here. OK? Can you please give me his cell number?"

She looked at me with the same tight-mouthed, annoyed expression that I give sometimes. This day was so weird.

Outside, Andrew was working up a sweat playing basketball. Kevin was pretty good at it. I waved my phone in the air, and Andrew walked to the door. I said, "I'll call their dad while you finish your game."

I tried his cell, but it went to voice mail. "Hello, Mr. Leighton. This is Phoebe Spring. There's an emergency at your house. I need for you to call me back as soon as you get this."

Andrew said, "If you wait here for his call, I'll go pick up some groceries at ShopRite." He got out his keys. "And, Peebes, see if you can get the kids hosed down," making a yuck face.

273

"Brittney, can you come into the kitchen, please," I called. She scuffed up the stairs, chewing a wad of gum.

"I'm starved. There's nothing to eat around here," she said.

"Yeah." I looked over at Keira slumped on the couch with a cigarette in one hand and an empty glass in the other. "Andrew'll be back in a little while with lunch for you guys. I need you to get in the shower with soap and find some shampoo to wash your hair, too. Then Kevin's next. No lunch till you're cleaned up."

"Do I have to?" she whined as I edged her into the bathroom and closed the door.

I yelled, "And get some clean clothes on." I waited till I heard the water running.

Kevin eventually came upstairs, and stared. "Mom said you're my half sister, right? Where do you live?"

I smiled. "In Maple Ridge, NY. I'm in high school there."

"So, are you and Andrew doin' it?"

I looked down at him. "That's really rude. Your sister's done. Your turn, mister," as I pointed to the bathroom.

I followed Brittney to her room and looked around. It probably was nice at some point, but that was hard to see now. There wasn't an empty space on the floor, and I didn't want to look too close. Her closet was a mess, but she found a clean outfit and threw her dirty clothes on top of the heap. I just shook my head and left her to get dressed.

I heard the water running and yelled to Kevin, "No lunch till your hair's clean, too."

He ignored me and started singing something.

I found glasses and napkins in the kitchen and heard Andrew coming in. "Did he call back?" he asked quietly.

"Not yet. Who do we call in case he doesn't come?" I said, glancing at Keira who was snoring.

"Let's give it another hour, at least till the kids are fed."

My phone buzzed. "Hello, Mr. Leighton?" as Andrew unpacked two bags of groceries.

"Did you say there was an emergency? Who are you?" he asked.

"I'm Phoebe Spring, Keira's daughter from her first marriage. It's not why I called you. You're needed at the house. You're wife is passed out, and the kids have no food. When will you be here?"

"Jesus. She's drinking you said?"

"A lot. Where are you, Mr. Leighton? Your kids need you."

"I'm on a business trip, but I should be able to get back there in about two hours," he said.

"Is there a friend I can call to stay with Brittney and Kevin till you get here?"

"Let me think. There's a baby sitter…" I cut him off.

275

"An adult should be here, Mr. Leighton, not some kid. I can wait a couple of hours, but no longer. If you're not here, I'm calling the police."

I helped Andrew clear off the kitchen table and set out a big salad with a choice of tuna fish, chicken or roast beef sandwiches. I grabbed one and put it on the coffee table in front of Keira. She could eat it or not when she woke up.

I needed to talk to Mom, and she picked up right away. I said, "You were so right, Mom. She's here, drunk and passed out, but we're gonna stay until her husband gets here."

"I should have gone with you," she said.

"Actually, Andrew was a huge help with the younger boy. I'll call you when we're on the way back."

Brittney sat down at the table and finished her sandwich quickly. Kevin was in the kitchen about four minutes later, wolfing his first one down. I poured a glass of water for him as he waved off the salad. "What else you got?" he said.

"Help yourself," as I pointed to the fridge.

After they finished, we gave each kid a Klondike bar and sat down to talk.

"How long's it been since you've had a meal?" Andrew asked.

Kevin and Brittney looked at each other. "Lunch yesterday at school, and we ate the last of the peanut butter this morning," Kevin said.

"Your dad's coming," I said.

"Yeah? All right!" Kevin jumped up. "I've got some games downstairs. You wanna come, Andy?"

"It's Andrew. What're you playing?" as he followed Kevin.

Brittney seemed OK to sit with me and asked, "So what's going to happen now?"

"Does your mom do this often?"

She looked away. "If there's food in the house, I can cook OK for Kevin and me, or we eat PB and J."

"Have you told your dad this?"

"Well, he moved out a month ago. That's when Mom started getting really bad."

A little more than an hour later the kids both ran outside when they heard their dad pull in the driveway. Seeing for myself how my half brother and sister were growing up made me shudder to think I might have been here with them. No wonder Mom and Dad kept this from me.

Mr. Leighton waved us over. His business suit complimented his short but trim build. He said, "I'm Keith. Nice to meet you, and, by the way," he said looking at me closely, "the resemblance is incredible, especially to Brittney. Thanks for waiting."

I said, "I texted photos to you of how we found the kids and the house today. The kids told us you've been gone a month."

He said, "I saw the pictures, and I phoned the police after you called. They should be here soon to put this on record. I had no idea it was so bad. A month ago when I left, I thought she could pull herself together, but after seeing this, I need to get full custody. Then after you called, it occurred to me you might like to see Kevin and Brittney again. I would hope on a better day, though. Would you mind my calling you?"

I answered, "Maybe later on. I don't want to see Keira."

"Please keep my number and my business card," as he handed it to me. "And thanks, Phoebe, for the pictures and for feeding them. Kevin said you brought a feast. That should help my case."

We waved to Brittney and Kevin, and was surprised that Kevin ran to us. "Wait, are you coming back again?" he asked Andrew.

I was so reluctant to get involved, but these kids, only a little younger than I am, were dealing with their own family breakup. If they wanted me around, I could make an effort, just like Drew had done for me.

I said, "If you want to, but you should ask Brittney first."

On our way home Andrew said, "It's a good thing you went there this weekend. Those kids were on their own. Not a pretty sight."

I felt tears coming. Angrily, I said, "Keira is a walking zombie nightmare. She sucks the life out of everyone she touches it seems, and then moves on to the next victim."

"Don't even think about her. She may have been your birth mother, but not your real mother. Keith seems like he'll follow through with taking over. Sad situation though."

"I'm done with her and I've never felt so lucky in my life. Dad got me away from Keira. He didn't forget about me or Mom, for that matter."

"I won't forget about you, Phoebe," Andrew said before we kissed goodbye. "I'll see you next weekend. Jeff might be coming, too, if Sharon's interested."

"Hey, I should have thought of that," as I gave him one last kiss.

Mom must have heard Andrew's car leaving, because she came outside. I kept her close as we went over what happened. She said, "For your sake, I hoped she had changed. I can feel your disappointment."

"More like disgust, Mom. She did it all over again, screwing up two more kids. I realize why you didn't tell me about her."

"I just wanted to protect you, Phoebe. You've grown up so much in the last couple of months, making your own decisions, not always the best ones, but they're your mistakes to make. This fearless streak you show reminds me of myself at your age, but I have limits, young lady. You're fifteen, not twenty, and you have to keep me in the loop. I'll be starting back to work on Monday, and even though I won't be home until six or so, I want to know what's going on with you."

"That's the best news all day! You loved your job. We'll try not to keep important things from each other. OK?" I said, fearing I might have to be the one to tell her about Dad's new fling Drew and I saw the week before. "Maybe we could have Sharon and her mom over tomorrow and celebrate? We can help cook."

She answered, "OK, remember Drew's coming too."

I called to ask Sharon for dinner, and we made riding plans for Friday after school. Then I called Dad. He picked up.

"Well, how's my girl?"

I said, "Saw Keira, and it went downhill from there," and told the rest of the sorry afternoon events.

"That's very sad that Keira never got better, but what about the boy and girl? Are you going to stay in touch?"

"Probably too soon to say and only if they want me to, Dad. Their father seemed very nice, and caring. I just want to stay out of it for now."

Dad asked, "How about we have dinner this week, PS. I promise I won't make an excuse this time."

I replied, "Wednesday at the Black Duck would be good," and we signed off.

That's when it hit me. Today had probably been one of the worst days ever, but at this moment, I couldn't have been happier.

Melissa Verdier is retired after enjoying a long career of teaching Art. She lives in beautiful coastal Connecticut with her husband of many years and her rescue dog.

74635821R00157

Made in the USA
Middletown, DE
28 May 2018